W9-BSR-886

Other Books by William Sleator

Rewind

The Boxes

The Beasties

The Night the Heads Came

Dangerous Wishes

Oddballs

The Spirit House

Others See Us

Strange Attractors

The Duplicate

The Boy Who Reversed Himself

Singularity

Interstellar Pig

Fingers

The Green Futures of Tycho

Into the Dream

Among the Dolls

House of Stairs

Run

Blackbriar

BOLTZMON!

BOLTZMON!

WILLIAM SLEATOR

DUTTON CHILDREN'S BOOKS • NEW YORK

Library of Congress Cataloging-in-Publication Data
Sleator, William. • Boltzmon!/by William Sleator.—1st ed. p. cm.
Summary: A boltzmon, remnant of a black hole, materializes in eleven-year-old Chris's bedroom and transports him to a parallel world, where he encounters the bitter woman his overbearing older sister will become, after his death, if he cannot convince her to change. • ISBN 0-525-46131-0 (hc)
[1. Brothers and sisters—Fiction. 2. Space and time—Fiction.]
I.Title. PZ7.S6313Bm 1999 [Fic]—dc21 99-34468 CIP

Published in the United States by Dutton Children's Books,
a division of Penguin Putnam Books for Young Readers
345 Hudson Street, New York, New York 10014
http://www.penguinputnam.com/yreaders/index.htm

Designed by Alan Carr • First Edition
1 3 5 7 9 10 8 6 4 2

For Lep

BOLTZMON!

chapter 1

The boltzmon arrived on the night Lulu threw her horrific slumber party.

Lulu's my nasty older sister. Her bedroom was the whole third floor of our house. Mom was always telling Dad he spoiled her, and the refinished attic was a perfect example. The Saturday night of the slumber party, the shrieking up there was so out of control, and the pounding music so loud, that I *almost* couldn't concentrate.

But I was mentally in Arteria. And when I put my mind there, I could blot out nearly everything else.

I sat in my room on the second floor, at the computer, working on a map of my imaginary country. I had named it Arteria after its many branching rivers. What interested me about it was its geography. I made it tropical because I was fascinated by the tropics, the fact that it never got cold there—I was frail and hated the cold—and was enthralled by pictures I had seen of dense tropical blooming vegetation and mysterious jungles. I loved mapping out the intricate rivers, some big and brown and sluggish, others racing at the bottom of gorges. I loved constructing its mountain range, and the jungle below the mountains.

In the jungle live cannibal bandits who have a special taste for eating blondes.

"Who said that?" I whispered to myself. It was like a voice inside my head. But I liked the idea. Lulu was blonde. Lulu had always picked on me, and tonight she and her friends were making some terrible noise upstairs. I quickly created a location for the bandit camp, deep in the dark green jungle.

The bandits would be filthy and vicious and loud—unlike the ordinary poor Arterian people, who were gentle and soft-spoken. I loved putting in the bandits because they were a way of mentally getting back at Lulu.

What else about Arteria that fascinated me, aside from the geography, were the structures I called the Time Temples. They were far from the large fork in the Aortazon River where the boat to Arteria landed, on the other side of the dangerous jungle. You had to go through the jungle to get to the Time Temples because they were very powerful, and that power had to be earned. I wasn't exactly sure what their power was, except that it had to do with the future and the past, and, anyway, I liked the name, *Time Temples.*

Did you know that you will die if you don't get to the Time Temples as soon as possible?

I slapped my hand over my ear. Why had I suddenly come up with *that* scary idea? It was like a voice inside my head again. How could I ever get to a place on a computer map?

The noise from upstairs had to be distracting me after all; that's why my mind was wandering. Mom called up to me. The party must be disturbing her, too, and she was working all the way down in her study on the first floor.

I went to the top of the stairs. "What did you say?"

"Go up there and tell those girls to keep it down or I'll kill them!" Mom yelled from the bottom of the stairs.

I didn't want to complain to Lulu—she had a nasty temper. "You think they'll listen to me?" I objected.

"Tell them it's an order from me," Mom insisted. "Tell them they'll all have to go home if they don't turn down that music and stop acting like wild savages."

Wild savages. That made me think of the bandits—the bandits who liked eating blondes like Lulu. I smiled a little.

She was thirteen—two years older than me—and always bossing me around. I was nervous about giving her an order in front of her friends—especially since I had just found out about the rotten thing she had done to me at school.

I pounded on the attic door—I didn't want to just walk in on a bunch of girls—but the music was so loud they couldn't hear it. I pushed the door open and started up. The stairs were vibrating from the bass of Lulu's stereo.

I stopped on the small dark landing where the steps turned; it was piled with cardboard boxes that were filled with old magazines and other junk. I would yell at them from there instead of barging in on them. I opened my mouth.

And then I choked. A spherical eye floated just in front of the Res-Q-Ladder box, staring at me.

"That shade looks great on you, Sally. Can I see how it looks on me?" Lulu brayed over the music.

I couldn't turn away from the eye, which seemed to be alive. I was too stunned even to scream. The eye pivoted and winked at me with a gooey eyelid. Then suddenly it shrank down to a pale glowing silver ball about the size of my fingernail, hanging there.

"Just a second, I'm still putting it on," Lulu's friend said.

"Okay, take your time," Lulu answered. If she'd been talking to me, it would have been an order to hand it over.

But I wasn't thinking about that now. My heart was thudding hard. A floating eyeball? But frightened as I was, I reached out and grabbed the little silver ball. I didn't know what it was, if it was good or evil, scary or wonderful. But I did know it was magical. And if Lulu knew about it, she'd want it. And she'd get it.

It was icy cold in my hand. I slipped it into my shirt pocket. "Hey!" I called up the stairs. I was scared of going up there—and now that I had found this thing, whatever it was, I was even more reluctant to confront Lulu. "Mom says you have to—"

"Okay, here's your lipstick!" Lulu's friend shouted.

They couldn't hear me. I trudged up the stairs and stopped just at the top.

Lulu had wanted pink, she had wanted frilly, and Dad, who was an interior designer, had given it to her. Everything was the color of bubble gum—the walls, the thick carpet, the checked curtains, the bedspread and pillowcases. I never went up there; all that screaming pinkness made me feel sick. Anyway, Lulu didn't want me to go up there—especially not now.

"What are you doing here, filth?" she demanded as soon as I reached the top of the steps. "Who invited you? Butt out!" Her voice was completely different from the one she used with her friends.

Lulu glared. Her friends stared dumbly at her, as if they couldn't believe how she talked to me. Their faces were all smeared with makeup—savages in ruffled nightdresses.

I tried to keep my voice steady. "Er, Mom asked me to tell you to please keep the noise down or else—"

"Tell Mom to come up if she wants to talk to me, jerk!"

That wasn't smart of her. I could smell cigarette smoke.

Something squirmed in my pocket. I grabbed for it, too late: They saw the slippery purple blob oozing out of my pocket and crawling down the front of my shirt. I folded my hand around it and shoved it back in.

Lulu's friends screamed. One of them cried, "A snake!"

But I bet Lulu didn't think it was a snake.

"Mom says everybody will have to go home if you don't quiet down," I said quickly, trying to distract her.

It worked. "Well, Mom has to tell me that herself!"

As usual, I couldn't argue with her. "Okay. I tried," I said, and started down, eager to get out of there. Who knew what this thing in my pocket was going to do next?

"Hey, wait a minute! What was that thing in your—"

I hurried down and shut the door behind me.

My earliest memory of Lulu: some southern vacation. Mom and Dad fussing over me and ignoring Lulu until Lulu offers to take me for a walk. "Time for a little rest," she says, and sits me down on a large pile of pineapple peelings, probably a garbage dump. Down I go on the sticky-sweet pineapple. Along come the ants—stinging red ones. I scream and scream. Mom and Dad yell at Lulu. She cries and says that she didn't know, she just wanted to take care of me. Later, when Lulu picks me up, Mom pulls me away from her.

Another vacation, a year or so later: I'm on the beach building a sand castle. In my memory the castle is elaborate and turreted, though it probably was more primitive than I remember, but Mom and Dad say it's beautiful. I feel very proud, strutting, because all Lulu can make are stupid impressions of upside-down buckets, which Mom and Dad ignore. When they are busy elsewhere, Lulu kicks my castle apart.

Even though Lulu is two years ahead of me in school, it was clear from the beginning that I was the better student. I was happy and excited on report card days when Mom and Dad would praise me and be disappointed in Lulu.

But she could turn that around, too. She always had a clique of dumb, noisy girls around her, and she would say to me, "Is the computer your only friend? Are you going to spend your life in front of it drawing useless maps of those stupid imaginary countries you care about so much?"

"You can hardly even write your name on the computer," I dared to say.

"You're just a freaky weirdo!" she spat at me.

It got worse when Lulu entered middle school. Suddenly everything was boys and makeup. "*Please* make yourself scarce when my friends come over, Chrissikins, dear," Lulu said, thinking she was sounding grown-up and sophisticated. "I don't want you embarrassing me." Of course she never said things like that in front of Mom and Dad.

I had friends. Mark and Larry and I went to the movies and hung out after school sometimes. But at home, where it was necessary for me to spend most of my time, Lulu became more and more of a cold-blooded tyrant. The only peace I had was when she and Dad were off playing golf, but when they came back she would put me down for having no interest in the game, and Dad didn't disagree with her.

Mom stood up for me when she was around. But she spent a lot of time at the university and was always going out of town to meetings, and she was closed off in her study working when she was at home, too, so she was not often there to defend me.

The school year had started a couple of months before the pivotal boltzmon slumber party.

Now I was in sixth grade, just starting middle school, and Lulu was in eighth, at the top of the heap. Lulu was pretty, a big wheel, a cheerleader, and active in the student council. She was also starting to hang out with some of the tougher kids.

I was intimidated by the much larger school and all the big older kids. I didn't expect Lulu to be at all friendly to me, and she wasn't. She behaved as though she didn't know who I was.

And then I began to notice kids looking away from me and giggling in the hallways, or whispering pointedly when I entered a classroom.

One day after school I caught up with Larry, who was pretending he didn't see me. "Hey, I don't want to sound like I'm imagining things, but are kids saying weird things about me?" I asked him. I hadn't seen much of him recently, for some reason.

"Er, I don't think so," he said, embarrassed.

"They must be, or you wouldn't be acting like that," I said to him. "Come on. I won't tell anybody you told me."

We were walking past the abandoned fire department practice rescue tower, an old structure made out of cast iron and stained, crumbling cement. I knew kids had gotten beaten up there, and I avoided it, but Larry was going that way.

He looked away. "Oh, well, maybe some kids are saying things about you. *I* don't believe them."

"Like what?"

He still wouldn't meet my eye. "Like you can't go to sleep unless your Mom reads you a bedtime story."

"What else?"

He sighed. "And . . . you won't stop sucking your thumb, at the age of eleven. And . . ." He sighed.

"Out with it."

"And wetting the bed," he blurted out. "I know you don't. But it's like everybody *wants* to believe it."

I was stung, like my gut was being yanked from the inside. Of course I knew who had started these stories.

"Thanks for letting me know," I said. "And don't worry, you don't have to walk home with me." Not that he'd walked home with me for a while anyway.

That was the Friday before Lulu's slumber party. Mom and Dad went out to a dinner, and Lulu had been shut up in her room since she got home from school. I didn't say anything to Mom and Dad about the lies Lulu was spreading about me at school. She would just deny it, and Dad would believe her. Mom might get a little angry at Lulu, but it wouldn't change anything. Nothing would.

I had just started sixth grade, and she was already turning me into an outcast. And more than ever I wondered why. What had I done to her?

I didn't know how to fight her, I just wasn't like that. I had to face the fact that I was a dumb jerk who let his older sister win every time.

I ate my frozen dinner and went up to my room. At least I had Arteria—with its beautiful branching rivers and powerful, mysterious Time Temples—to escape into. But I did leave the door of my room open. I knew she would have to go past when she came down to microwave her frozen dinner. And around seven o'clock the attic door opened and she walked past, not looking at me.

I felt so humiliated I actually said, "Lulu, can't we call a truce? Do you have to spread stories about me? Isn't just ignoring me enough?"

"I don't know what you're talking about," she said. "Don't bother me now. I'm hungry."

"Mom and Dad might be interested to hear about the stories you're telling about me at school," I said, hurting, knowing I could never tell them.

"That's just what I'd expect from a tattletale mama's boy

like you, always trying to impress her!" she snapped. Then she smiled. "I can't help it if the kids at middle school think you're peculiar. I knew it would be like that. What do you *expect* normal kids to think about you? You're lucky they're not beating you up, like they did to those other sixth-graders. I swear, I will never understand how I ended up with a brother like you." And she walked away, still smiling.

And I was wondering how I had ever ended up with a sister like her. And the worst of it was, it would just go on like this, getting more and more painful. How was I going to survive middle school?

And there was absolutely nothing I could do about it.

The next night I hurried downstairs from Lulu's room in the middle of her party, clutching at the object in my shirt pocket, the object that kept magically changing shape. I went all the way down to the first floor—the stairs felt different with the thick new carpeting.

"Lulu won't pay any attention to me," I enjoyed telling Mom. "She says she won't quiet down until she hears it from you." I was hoping Mom would go upstairs and smell the cigarette smoke.

"She expects me to stop working and go all the way up there?" she said angrily, starting to get up. "I'm sending those kids home this—"

Lulu's stereo suddenly got much, much quieter. Mom sat down. I was disappointed that she wasn't going to break up the party. "She just didn't want to do it in front of me, with her friends there," I said. "She never gives in to me about anything."

Mom put her hand on my shoulder, meeting my eye. "I know it's hard, Chris," she said. "It'll be easier when she gets over whatever it is she's going through with you." She glanced down. "Why do you have your hand over your heart?"

I was trying to keep the strange object from squirming out of my pocket and revealing itself as it had done up in Lulu's room. "Er, just a little out of breath, I guess," I said, backing out of the room.

I hurried upstairs, knowing Mom was wrong about Lulu—Lulu wouldn't get over it; she would be out to get me as long as she breathed.

I went into my room and closed the door. At least the thing hadn't done anything funny in front of Mom. I reached tentatively into my shirt pocket, not knowing what I was going to find there, scared and excited at the same time.

I pulled out a little flake of grayish ash.

Yes, not much to look at, am I, when I'm not up to my cute tricks, a voice said inside my head. *But this is the real me, the boltzmon. I'm the remnant of a giant black hole from the future. I absorbed many galaxies, in this universe and others. I contain all the information ever absorbed into the black hole, libraries unimaginably vast. I know every-*

thing that ever has happened in this galaxy, and everything that ever will happen. I know that in 3.2 billion years this sun will go supernova and this planet will be toast.

"But why did you come here and—" I started to say.

You do not have my permission to interrupt. I am an extremely unstable particle. I have infinite states. If perturbed in a certain way, I will implode, vanishing into another universe—and dragging you along with me. In fact, I was quite deeply perturbed by that gaggle of debased adolescent females up there near where I found you. Perturbed enough to want to pop over to the next universe—taking you with me.

I was terrified. "But wait a minute! Maybe I don't want . . . I mean, how long will it take, how will we get back, what will Mom and Dad do, why did you pick me?" I remembered the earlier voice inside my head and felt even more scared. "Was it you who told me I would die if I didn't get to the Time Temples as soon as possible?"

I am indifferent to you. And now I really am *perturbed.*

The room went fuzzy and trembly, like a bad TV picture. And then it shrank away to nothing.

chapter 4

It was a flat wooden boat, dangerously low in the water and very crowded—most of the two dozen or so people on board were standing. The old timbers creaked as the boat rocked in the current of the river. The sun beat down; the heat was like an oven.

I felt dazed. Was this real?

I was standing next to a frail, elderly woman. Her clothes were ragged, and she smelled bad. That was real enough. I started to move away from her.

"Hey, now, wait just a minute, kid," the old woman whispered in a cracked, muffled voice with a strange accent. "I brought you here, and I want you to help me out."

"But it was the boltzmon who brought me," I whispered.

"Yes, I did, and don't you forget it," the woman said.

"I'm old and weak and hot. I feel faint. Look over there." She pointed.

One part of the boat was covered by a cloth awning, a small comfort area of shade from the glaring sunlight. We were standing quite near it, but not under it. There was a bench under the shade, and men and women were sitting on it—they must have boarded the boat before we did. A blond woman with a horsey face and way too much makeup sat almost at the end of the bench nearest to us, smoking. And next to her—on the bench, under the shade—was a fancy leather bag with some kind of logo on it. All the other bags were piled on the deck.

"Hey, that's lousy," I said, suddenly feeling outraged. "How can she put her *bag* on the bench in the shade, when you have to stand in the sun?"

"You got it, sonny," the boltzmon lady said, her voice weak. "If you know what you're doing, you can go now."

"Do they speak English here?" I asked her.

"That woman is American."

I wondered about that as I marched across the uneven wooden deck over to the too blond woman, who looked oddly familiar, despite the strangeness of everything. She was wearing pink shorts and a pink waist pack, and she really *could* have been American, like a lot of other people on the boat.

But there were also people dressed in wraparound skirts, both men and women, the women's longer than the men's. Some of these people had flowers in their dark hair. Where *were* we, anyway? This place reminded me of something, but I couldn't figure out exactly what.

"Excuse me," I said to the blond woman whose fancy bag was on the bench in the shade. I was intimidated by her, but I knew the boltzmon was very important, if it had the power to bring me to this strange place—it had proved that it spoke the truth. "The woman I'm with is old and weak, and she needs a cool place to sit."

The blond woman stared straight ahead as though I didn't exist, puffing on her cigarette. Her dyed blond hair gave the impression of wild disarray, yet every strand was stiff and unmoving in the breeze.

"I think my friend might faint or get sick if she doesn't sit down soon," I continued.

The woman still didn't look at me. But the other people on the bench were watching and listening now.

"The bench in the shade is for people, right?" I went on. "Everybody else's bags are on the deck."

She finally turned and looked at me. "This is a Prada bag," she said loftily, a queen speaking to a peasant.

I didn't know what Prada meant, but now I knew that this woman was not the kind of person who listened to reason. She needed to be told what to do. I was scared to do it, but I knew the boltzmon lady mattered more than my own fears—and I was more scared of her than of the blonde. "Whatever a Prada is, it's not as important as a person," I said hesitantly. "Could you, uh, please put that bag on the deck like everybody else, so my friend can sit down?"

"The boy is right," said the young man sitting next to her. He had a big red flower in his dark hair, and a gentle voice.

The blonde turned to him angrily. "Well, you can just butt out of—"

"Do not talk to my son in that way," said the middle-aged woman next to the man.

Other people—the strangely dressed ones—chimed in:

"Yes! Yes!"

"They are right."

"Put your bag on the deck."

I was cheering inside.

The blonde's eyes widened; she seemed startled, even a little frightened. She grabbed for her bag, glaring at me. Then she looked away and sullenly and ungraciously moved the bag onto the floor at her feet. "Thank you. You are so kind," I said. I went over and took the boltzmon lady's hand and helped her over to the bench, where she sat down.

The first thing she did was to lean forward and spit onto

the deck. The blonde recoiled in disgust, shielding her bag with her hands. The boltzmon woman leaned back comfortably.

I stood beside her in the shade, which was a lot more comfortable. She was dressed like the other foreign women, though the clothing hung loosely on her. I was also wearing a wraparound garment, but I didn't feel self-conscious because so many men were dressed the same way.

Now that she had a place to sit, I began to worry that the boat might sink. "Isn't this boat too low in the water? Do you think it's safe?"

"No," the boltzmon said flatly.

"But there aren't any life preservers," I said.

"What do you expect in a place like this?" she said, and spat on the floor again, closer to the blonde's feet. The blonde shuddered.

"Where are we, anyway?" I asked.

"Look around. You might recognize something."

"But how could I ever recognize anything in this weird place? I've never been here before."

She sighed impatiently. "Please try not to irritate me even more or I might lose control," she said in a frail but annoyed voice. "I could implode again at any instant, and we might end up someplace a lot farther away than this—and a lot harder to get back from, too. Look around, I told you."

I looked around.

The boat progressed slowly, rising and falling and sighing on the wide brown river. Palm trees taller than I had ever seen swayed gently on both sides of the water. It was beautiful here, with everything deeply green.

The right bank was almost too far away to see, but we were very close to shore on the left. I could see that the river branched off at frequent intervals into smaller tributaries, curving off into the underbrush, and that these branched off into even smaller streams.

I thought of something and looked quickly ahead. We were approaching a major fork in the large river, where there was a pier and a shed and a track leading into a jungle.

I felt my heart thudding. I turned back to the boltzmon woman, shivering in the intense heat. "Arteria?" I breathed. "Is this the Aortazon River?"

"You got it," she said. She was stretching out more comfortably on the bench, leaning sideways, forcing the obnoxious blonde, who didn't want to touch the smelly old lady, to squeeze more tightly against the other people, who were looking disgruntled about it.

"But Arteria isn't real," I said, very scared now. "It's just a place I made up. We can't really be *in* it!"

"Who says? Who says your brain couldn't have been influenced by what really *is* in the universe next door?"

The blonde carefully pulled her precious Prada bag

across the rough plank deck now, trying to get farther away from the almost reclining boltzmon woman. The other people on the bench were shooting hostile looks at the blonde, and nudging one another and whispering among themselves. They seemed to be blaming *her* for taking up too much space, not the old lady.

"So, you're saying that this is the universe next door, and somehow it influenced my mind, and that's why I drew the maps? Is it called Arteria here, too?"

"Do you always ask such dumb questions?" the boltzmon woman said testily. "Don't upset me, okay? It can be *very* dangerous." She sighed again. "We are on a planet that is exactly like Earth, except for two major differences. It has a country on it called Arteria, where we now are. And it is forty years ahead of Earth in time."

"And are the Time Temples at the end of that track? Do people really get killed trying to get to them?"

"*You* are going to get killed, back on your own world, if you don't get to those temples as soon as possible," the boltzmon woman casually told me. She stretched farther into the blonde's space.

"*What?*" I said, feeling the breath knocked out of me. It wasn't a complete surprise to hear this, but it was more terrifying now because the boltzmon had proved it spoke the truth. "It *was* you who told me that before!"

The boltzmon didn't respond; a lot was going on now. The blonde squeezed away from her, pressing against the young man next to her. "Hey, old lady. I let you sit down. Will you stop taking up so much space," the blonde complained to the boltzmon.

"You don't know who you're talking to, you dumb cluck. I'll sit any way I want," the boltzmon snapped at her.

"I'll push you off this bench if you don't give me more room!" the blonde threatened.

"It is very rude to speak to an old woman in that way," the young man next to the blonde reprimanded her.

"Leave the poor thing alone," said his mother.

"And please do not be squeezing so close to me," the young man said to the blonde.

"The old hag is the one who's taking up too much room, not me!" the blonde said, her voice rising.

"I am feeling *very* unstable," the boltzmon said.

I had to get to the Time Temples or I'd die—the boltzmon knew everything that was going to happen. But if this blond woman didn't calm down, the boltzmon would get disturbed to the breaking point and we'd flip-flop into some other universe and I'd never get to the temples at all.

"Excuse me," I said to the blonde. "Please be careful with this woman. She doesn't look it, but she's really powerful. If she gets upset, there'll be problems."

"I told you to move over, you disgusting old hag!" the blonde ordered the boltzmon.

This horrible woman was going to ruin everything. I'd never get to the temples because of her. "Please listen," I begged her. "You've got to be nice to her or else—"

"Butt out, brat!" the blonde shouted at me. With both hands she shoved the boltzmon off the bench. The boltzmon tumbled onto the deck, her old bones clattering as if they'd snap in two.

"No!" I screamed, quickly bending down to help the boltzmon, terrified of what she might do.

"The boat's sinking!" somebody shouted.

"You've done it! I'm perturbed! Here we go!" the boltzmon cried.

"Please don't take me away from here!" I begged her. "You said I'd die if I didn't get to the Time—"

But before I could even finish speaking, everything trembled and went black.

Where were we going to end up now?

In my room again, hearing music from the party upstairs. It hadn't brought me back much later than it was when we'd left.

I sank down onto my bed, panting, holding the piece of ash in my palm. I was relieved it had brought me back here instead of to some other universe. But I was very worried about getting to the Time Temples.

"Will we ever get back to Arteria again?" I asked. "How soon will I die if I don't get to the Time Temples?"

I don't feel like talking about it. Leave me alone.

I sighed. The blonde had been obnoxious, for sure. But the boltzmon hadn't helped much, either, by purposely provoking her. Maybe it knew everything, but it sure was hard to deal with.

I slipped it into my shirt pocket and sat down at the

computer. I had about one million questions to ask, but it wouldn't answer them now. What I *did* know was that I had to get to the temples.

And I knew exactly how to make that a whole lot easier. I started typing.

But before I got to my Arteria file Lulu barged into the room. "Where's my Prada bag?" she demanded.

"Your *what?*" I said, very surprised.

She sighed. "You know, my leather bag with the Prada logo on it. Dad gave it to me. It's very valuable. It's where I keep my most precious jewelry and makeup. And I can't *find* it!" She stamped her foot.

I couldn't help smiling, thinking of the blond woman and her Prada bag on the boat in Arteria. Come to think of it, that horrible woman was a lot like Lulu.

"What's so funny?" Lulu demanded. "You *did* steal it and hide it! Otherwise you wouldn't be smiling like that."

"I didn't even know you had that bag. You think I want something like that?" Normally I would have been afraid of her. Now I still couldn't stop smiling.

That enraged her. "You think things are tough for you at school now, huh?" she snarled. "Wait and see."

But I wasn't as intimidated by her as I had always been before. I remembered how I had talked to the blonde on the boat. "So now you admit telling lies about me?"

"Huh?" For a moment she didn't know what to say, she was so confused that I was standing up to her like this. Then she got it together. "Don't change the subject!" she ordered me. "Just give me back my bag!"

"Hey, hey, what's the problem here?" Dad said, coming into the room. He was a big sturdy guy with a round face and blond hair.

Lulu's manner changed abruptly. Now she wasn't angry and threatening, she was all wounded innocence. "Chris took my Prada bag, my favorite thing in the whole world because *you* gave it to me," she whimpered. "And he's hiding it and won't tell me where."

Dad frowned. "Give her back her bag, Chris. Now."

"But, Dad, I don't have it. You know I don't do things like that. Why would I make trouble? Look around, in my closet, in my drawers. I don't have any bag like that." I stood up and opened my closet door. I pulled out the drawers of my bureau. Lulu didn't hesitate to look. And she didn't find her bag.

"Well, then he hid it somewhere else," Lulu said. "It would be too obvious to hide it in his own room."

The boltzmon was sliding around in my pocket now. Could they see the movement through the cloth? What was it going to turn into this time? Why did it keep revealing itself when other people were around?

"I've never taken any of your things before, Lulu," I said. "Why should I start tonight? You probably just left the bag somewhere and forgot, because you're too flaky to remember where your things are. Did you look anywhere else before you came in here to accuse me?"

"That's not a very nice way to talk to your sister," Dad said, his scowl deepening.

That was too much. Lulu was being nasty, not me. I remembered how the blonde on the boat had given in about moving her bag when I had insisted, logically and calmly. "Well, it's not very nice of Lulu to spread lies about me at school, when she knows everybody and I'm just starting out. You can ask her friends upstairs about the things she says."

Lulu's mouth dropped open. She had thought I would never dare to tell them. I had thought so, too. But I had just done it.

I felt the boltzmon rolling around against my chest.

"My daughter would never—" Dad started to say.

"I've been listening to this conversation for the last five minutes," Mom said from the doorway. "Lulu, you left that ridiculously expensive bag in the hall closet when you came home from showing it off at school yesterday, and it's still down there." She turned to me. "What's this about Lulu telling stories about you at school?"

Now I wished I hadn't said anything. I had thought it would be brave of me to tell what she had done, but now I knew it wasn't; I *was* being a little mama's boy tattletale, just as Lulu had said last night.

And Mom was serious; Lulu was going to get into real trouble, and she would take it out on me in some even more horrible way. I put my hand over my pocket to keep the writhing boltzmon inside. "Oh, nothing. Forget it. It was just—"

"Don't back down, Chris," Mom said firmly. "Tell us."

It was so babyish, telling this to my parents, but how could I get out of it now? My hand still over my pocket, I said, "That Mom has to read me bedtime stories before I can go to sleep, that I suck my thumb, and . . . wet the bed. It's all over the whole school. Ask her friends upstairs. Even my own friends believe it and won't hang out with me."

"He's lying!" Lulu shouted, her face red.

"We'll see," Mom said in an icy voice. "Up we go." She herded Lulu and Dad out of the room. I remembered the smell of cigarettes in Lulu's room. She was really going to get it. And then I would get it even worse.

I lifted my hand from my pocket.

A reptilian thing hopped out of my pocket onto the desk, a head with two froglike legs and greenish mottled skin. The one eye in the middle of its forehead winked at me, and the very wide, lipless mouth opened. "Your father and sister are maddening," it peeped.

"You almost made it a lot worse by jumping around in my pocket when they were in here. If Lulu finds out about you, she'll take you away from me." I sighed, ashamed of myself for telling on Lulu and worried about how Lulu was going to get back at me. "Why do you keep almost revealing yourself?"

"Why do I keep almost revealing myself, you ask me," the boltzmon said. I could tell by the sound of its little voice that if it could have shrugged, it would have. "I told you, I have infinite states. Sometimes I just get these impulses. Sometimes they are impossible to resist."

"But what are you doing here? Why did you come to me?"

"A whim."

I sighed and shook my head. And then I thought of something really chilling. "You said I would die if I didn't get to the Time Temples right away. You said you know everything that ever happened and ever will happen. So how am I going to die? And when?"

"Questions, questions," the boltzmon said, flopping around on my desk as if my deadly concern didn't matter at all.

I heard a lot of footsteps coming down the stairs. Lulu's

friends were being sent home. This was going to be really, really bad.

"But what's going to happen to me? And when?" I whispered.

"That would be telling," said the boltzmon unhelpfully, jumping on and off a textbook, like someone doing step aerobics. "You sound perturbed," it said pleasantly.

"You're not going to *tell* me?" I said, with a horrible sinking feeling.

The boltzmon, nothing but a head with two legs, was now singing "Ga, ga, ga!" and hopping on one foot and kicking the other one in the air, like a manic deformed cancan dancer.

I was going to have to help myself. I started typing, desperate to log onto Arteria and get rid of the bandits. I wasn't blond, I had dark hair and eyes like Mom, but that didn't mean the cannibal bandits weren't a threat to me. Without the bandits, if we ever really got back to Arteria again, it wouldn't be so difficult to get to the Time Temples. I could also put the temples closer to the river, so the jungle trek wouldn't be so long.

"I wouldn't bother fussing around with that primitive little stone-age tool," the boltzmon said, still dancing, sounding a little out of breath. "It won't change anything."

I lifted my hands from the keyboard. "What do you mean?"

"Arteria is the way it is. That thing can't change it. I told you, it's in the universe next door, and you sensed what it was like—with a little help from me. And that's the way it's always going to be."

"You mean . . . I've got to go through the jungle, and deal with the bandits, and—"

"Ga, ga, ga!" sang the boltzmon, dancing wildly.

I was so angry I reached over and picked it up and squeezed it. "Why aren't you helping me?"

It grinned with its wide lipless mouth. "Temper, temper. I might get upset again," it said.

"*I'm* upset!" I said. "You told me I'd die if I didn't get to the Time Temples."

"And it's the truth, too."

"Then you have to tell me how I'm supposed to die, and how to get to the Time Temples, as fast as possible."

"You can't make demands like that of me!" the boltzmon said, its little peep of a voice sounding angry. "I'm the remnant of a giant black hole. I know everything that ever happened and everything that ever will happen. I have infinite degrees of freedom. You're nothing but a human."

"I thought you were here to help me, but you're just making everything worse."

"Here to help you?" The boltzmon was slithering around impatiently in my sweaty hand. "Why should I *help* you? I'm just here to have fun! How dare you suggest I'm your . . . your servant, or slave, or some kind of genie."

"Sorry. Can you please help me save my life?"

"I'll do anything I feel like. And right now, *you* are infuriating me. Here to help you indeed! You shouldn't have said that, boy." It was getting bigger and heavier, its voice deepening. "Put me down!"

I put it down, fast. "Sorry. Please forget I said that. I apologize. Please."

It was lolling on the desk, ballooning up into a kind of spongy, foamy mass. *I am perturbed. Perturbed enough to implode. And you are coming with me.*

"No! Stop!" I begged it.

Everything went fuzzy, and then black.

It was mad at *me* now. What terrible place was it going to drag me to?

chapter 6

The boat had reached the landing dock on the left bank of the Aortazon, and it was sinking.

The passengers, many of them drenched, were climbing off over the railing wherever they could as the boat sank more quickly, gurgling. I was the last one off. The boltzmon woman must have gotten off the boat already. Typical of the thing not to wait for me, or to try to help me.

But I was back in Arteria! My heart flooded with relief. I had been afraid the boltzmon was going to punish me and drag me to some horrible universe, but instead it had taken me to exactly where I wanted to be. Maybe it wasn't so bad after all.

We could start off for the Time Temples right away.

The people ahead of me were going up a flight of rickety steps into a shack built on poles over the water. I followed them, hoping to find the boltzmon there. I wanted to be in Arteria, but I didn't know if I really wanted to be here alone, without the boltzmon's powers—not that it had helped much last time.

Inside the hot room a man in a brown uniform sat behind a littered wooden counter. People were showing him documents, and he was writing things down. There was no orderly line; people just thronged around the counter.

All I had put on my map was a boat landing and a shed. So where had all this other stuff come from? Maybe it was because Arteria was real, and the map I had made was only a partial image of it—in the same way that an ordinary road map of a country doesn't tell you how the people there dress or what they eat, or what their customs are.

I looked around the room for the boltzmon.

The obnoxious blonde, who was soaking wet, was elbowing her way through, a wild look on her face, pushing past and squeezing between other people to get to the counter. The others were all gentler than she was.

I walked around the room, but I couldn't find the boltzmon.

Then I saw the man with the red flower in his hair who had been sitting next to the blonde, and his mother. The mother had a soft, pleasant face; the man was shirtless, wearing only a sarong. They might be nice people; they had defended me. "Excuse me," I said.

The woman smiled. "You are the boy who helped the old lady," she said.

"That's right," I said. "And now I can't find her. Did you see her? She's not in this room."

They shook their heads.

"But doesn't everybody have to go through here?" I asked him. "It looks like immigration or something."

"Only the people who are trying to get to the temples have to go through here," the woman told me. "They have to have a record of everybody who makes the trek, so they will know the names of those who die."

"So if the old lady isn't in here, that means she *isn't* going to the temples?" I said, with a sinking feeling. Did I dare to make the trip without the boltzmon? "The reason many people die—is it because of the bandits?" I asked them.

The man nodded. "There are dangerous animals, too. But the bandits, they are very, very terrible."

I hadn't put any dangerous animals in the jungle. That was another part of Arteria that wasn't on the map. How many other unpleasant surprises would there be?

"But the bandits prefer foreign flesh," the man said quickly. "Poor Arterians like us, without money or flesh they like, are much safer. Foreigners and rich Arterians take the bus, but it is still very dangerous. Perhaps they think the temples will give them youth. Come, almost all the rich people are gone now. We must see the inspector."

Why did they think I was Arterian? Maybe because I was dressed like them, and had dark hair. That might help protect me. It was lucky they spoke English—maybe the country had been a colony once.

I went along with them to the counter. I was afraid, but had no choice. Why had the boltzmon gone away from me? That was almost as scary as the bandits.

Only the blonde was still at the counter, puffing on a cigarette. "This is a valid passport," she was saying.

The inspector looked at the picture, then back up to her, frowning and shaking his head.

There were no pockets in my sarong. I didn't have a passport. If the inspector was giving the blonde trouble even though she *did* have a passport, then he wouldn't let me through, and I'd never get to the Time Temples. But I was still going to try.

"Who is the woman in this photograph?" the inspector asked the blonde.

"*Me!* Can't you see? Hurry, or I'll miss the bus."

He shook his head. "The woman in this picture is much too young to be you," the inspector said.

The blonde's skin was leathery and wrinkled; she looked

as if she spent too much time in the sun and smoked a lot. Her blond hair was dark at the roots and thin; it must have been bleached so much that a lot of it had fallen out.

"That picture was taken four years ago," she said.

"No one could have aged so much in only four years," the inspector said. I looked closely at him. There almost seemed to be a humorous glint in his eyes.

I peered down at the counter to see the blonde's picture. I couldn't help being curious about how much younger she had looked four years ago. I also wanted to see her name. She acted so much like Lulu. And the boltzmon had said this planet was forty years ahead in time.

"Hey, kid, you just butt out!" the blonde snapped at me before I had a chance to see the passport. "I'm ahead of you."

The inspector looked at me and at the mother and son. There was something familiar about his expression. "You three, you can go on through," he said, waving some papers casually. "There's a *gwian* and a driver waiting just outside, heading for the temples. Just tell me your names."

"Now wait just a minute!" the blonde burst out. "You didn't even *ask* to see *their* passports!"

"Thank you, sir," the young man said to the inspector. "My name is Awn and my mother is Sai."

"But this is *ridiculous*!" the blonde protested. "It's not fair!"

"Don't tell me how to run my business, woman," the inspector said to the blonde. "You are a very annoying person. Anyone can see those three are citizens of Arteria. They don't need passports. But people like you, foreigners with suspicious passports, can get in a lot of trouble. I warn you, don't get me angry."

It was too much for the blonde; she was losing control. "You're telling me my valid passport is no good and letting people *without* passports through? I want to see your supervisor."

"You are greatly perturbing me, woman," the inspector said, and now I knew who the inspector really was. "Please control yourself or there will be trouble. Your name, young man?" he asked me.

"Chris," I said.

"I don't believe this," the blonde said. She reached over the counter for her passport. "Give my passport back to me and let me through! I've got to catch that bus!"

The inspector—the boltzmon—whipped her passport behind his back. "I warn you, woman. Control yourself or you'll never get out of this village. We have a miserable prison here with very unpleasant toilets."

He turned to me again. "How do you spell your name?"

I could sense the boltzmon was about to go over the edge. When it imploded, what would happen to me this time? But the inspector's pen was still poised. "C-H-R-I-S,"

I said, fast, and he wrote it down with one hand, holding the blonde's passport behind his back with the other.

"Give me my passport!" the blonde bellowed, flinging her body over the counter and flailing her hands.

I ran for the door.

But it was too late. Everything went blurry and then blacked out.

Back in my room, the ash in my hand.

I gulped and sank back in my desk chair, shaking my head. "Gee, things happen fast with you," I mumbled.

Put me back in your pocket.

It was always the same. Whenever I had one million questions to ask it, it was too irritable to answer. And when I *did* get a chance to ask it things, its answers were mostly illogical and unhelpful. Was this thing a blessing or a curse?

It seemed to have brought me back soon after we had left, which was convenient. It was almost ten P.M. now.

I didn't understand why the boltzmon did what it did when we were in Arteria. First it had been a frail, old Arterian lady. Then it had been an immigration inspector. Why did it keep changing roles?

The first time the boltzmon had expected me to help it

by getting it a place to sit, and I had done it. Then it had pointlessly provoked the blonde to the point that she perturbed it and sent it imploding back here.

The second time the boltzmon had helped *me*, by letting me through without a passport. But again it had provoked the blonde, by withholding her passport, until her obnoxious behavior sent it imploding back here again. Would that pattern ever change? If it kept happening, we'd never be able to stay there long enough for me to get to the Time Temples. And then I'd be dead.

And most of all I wanted to know how I was going to die, and when. Why wouldn't the boltzmon tell me?

I had to get to the Time Temples in order to save myself, despite the wild animals and the bandits. But I didn't want to go now. I needed to rest, to sleep.

But the boltzmon was still in my shirt pocket. It wouldn't be safe there if Lulu came barging into the room, which she could easily do. The door didn't lock, Lulu was already suspicious about what was in my shirt pocket, and she was probably more furious at me than she had ever been in her life, blaming me for ruining her party.

I put the ash in the left shoe of an old pair of running sneakers at the bottom of a pile on my closet floor. Lulu had already been through my closet, looking for her bag, so maybe she wouldn't look there again when she sneaked into my room. And I was sure she'd be in here: Lulu would stop at nothing when she wanted to get back at me.

She came in the morning when I was still lying drowsily in bed. She didn't scream; her voice was ominously quiet. "You've really done it this time," she said, looking down at me, her face hard.

I sat up quickly, holding the covers up to my shoulders. I had no idea what to say to her.

She didn't need a response from me. "Tomorrow it will be all over the school that my little tattletale mama's boy brother broke up my party," she went on, her voice even and quiet. "That won't make me feel good at all, will it?"

"Wait a minute," I said. "If you hadn't—"

She turned and walked out the door.

And from that point on she behaved perfectly normally. She spent a lot of time up in her room practicing her pep talk for the student council school spirit assembly the next day. At supper she talked with Dad about golf swings and ignored me, which was her usual behavior. She certainly wasn't going to let Mom and Dad know that she was planning anything. And the way she had made her threat to me was so vague that I had nothing to link to her when something actually did happen.

Meanwhile, the boltzmon remained a silent gray ash in my sneaker. Since it wouldn't answer my questions, I tried to find some answers myself. I logged onto the Internet and activated a search to find any references to "boltzmon." All it could come up with was one scientific paper in an advanced theoretical physics journal, most of which I couldn't understand—stuff about quantum dynamics and preserving purity and the "t'Hooft anomaly." What I could understand was mostly just what the boltzmon had already told me: that it was a remnant of a black hole, containing all the information absorbed by the black hole. Because so much information was packed into such a tiny space, it had infinite states and was highly unstable, and, when perturbed—the article used that word!—it could disappear into another universe.

The article also said the boltzmon was infinitely degenerate and infinitely dense. I knew those words had scientific meanings, but if you looked at them in human terms, they also made sense. I shivered a little at the idea that the thing really *was* depraved—and I hoped it might be too dumb to get the better of me.

The only useful new information I learned was that the information the boltzmon contained consisted of not just the past and the future, but the DNA of all the living creatures and probably also the actual events that had occurred on the worlds absorbed by it. This stuff would be preserved forever within the boltzmon library. And because, as a black hole, the boltzmon had warped space and time, it would retain the ability to warp space and time.

Interesting, but it didn't stop me from worrying. The boltzmon still refused to respond when I went to bed Sunday night. Clearly it wasn't going to take me to Arteria before school on Monday. And what was Lulu going to do on Monday? Now it might be too late to get to the Time Temples and save myself.

It was a cold, overcast, late October day, and I was miserably tense on the way to school. I stayed tense all day, even though at first I didn't notice anything unusual at school. Of course people were whispering and avoiding me, but that was normal because of the lies Lulu had already spread about how babyish I was.

The assembly was after lunch. The student council officers, including Lulu, sat on stage looking proud of themselves. A couple of teachers made remarks about good citizenship and responsibility. Then Lulu got up.

Her pep talk started out like most of them did: how we should participate in school activities, be proud of our school, and support our teams. She acted cutely shy, smiling, her hands behind her back, swaying slightly in front of the mike. Then, at the end, she said very seriously, "We must *all* do our best to support our school. Students who do not—students who are different, not normal, students who do babyish things, who are sneaky, who are tattletales—students like this need our help to learn to change, to be more mature and not to be an embarrassment to our school. An embarrassment to our school is an embarrassment to every single one of us."

People near me were turning and looking at me now. Everyone knew she was talking about me. They were amazed she would go so far. Luckily, I was seated at the end of the aisle. I was out of there before her pep talk ended.

I had no idea what the kids would do to me now, but I wasn't going to wait around to find out. I went straight to the nurse's office and told her I had just thrown up. I assured her I lived very close to the school. She gave me a pass, and I was out of there and on my way home before the assembly was even over.

I had no choice but to ask the boltzmon for help. If I complained to Mom and Dad, Lulu would deny everything; she would say her speech had nothing to do with me. But what would the other kids do to "help" me learn not to be babyish? The tough kids at school only needed an excuse to pick on me, and Lulu had given them a big one. Other kids had gotten badly beaten for less reason than this.

I didn't know how going to the Time Temples could get me out of this mess, but I couldn't think of anything else to do. And I wanted to get to the Time Temples now, before I had to face the entire hostile student body tomorrow.

Mom and Dad were both at work, as usual, and Lulu was

still at school, and would be at cheerleading practice afterward. I closed the door of my room anyway. I dumped my books on my desk and picked up the old left shoe in my closet.

There was nothing in it.

I checked the right shoe, hoping I had remembered wrong. It was empty, too.

I sank down onto my bed, trying to fight off despair. It wasn't easy. There was nothing to prevent the boltzmon from just taking off and never coming back again. It had made it *very* clear that it was nothing like a genie that had to stick with me and obey my orders. It could do anything it wanted. And it had probably gotten bored here and hopped off to some other universe on a whim.

And if I didn't get to the Time Temples, what would happen at school tomorrow? Somehow, I knew the boltzmon had spoken the truth about my death—it could be evasive, but it didn't lie. Would it happen as a result of the kids at school responding to Lulu's speech? I could pretend to be sick and stay home, but not for long. Whatever they were going to do would happen soon.

I had been stupid to hope the boltzmon might help me. What had ever made me think it wasn't some kind of horrible evil spirit? The thing was degenerate for sure. It was all I could do not to cry.

I don't like it when little human beings think nasty things about me.

I jumped up from the bed, my heart thudding, hopeful again. "You're still here? Where are you?"

I didn't know there was anything wrong with your eyes.

I turned around and around, looking up and down. Where was it hiding?

And then I saw the mirror on the back of my door. But I didn't have a mirror on the back of my door. And yet, there I was in a mirror that had appeared out of nowhere. And in the mirror I didn't have a head. I stopped at my neatly sliced neck. I was holding a head in my arm, but it wasn't my head. It was the head of a woman. Her prominent cheekbones made her face diamond-shaped; the eyes slanted up at an unreal angle, the pupils vertical. She had pointed ears and frothy silver hair, and she was half smiling. She looked like a woman who had metamorphosed halfway into a lioness.

If you're that *unobservant, I don't know how you ever expect to get to the Time Temples,* the lion woman head in the mirror said in a deep female voice.

The boltzmon had taken the form of the mirror's world, and the image within it.

I gulped. I looked down at my arm. I was holding nothing in it in the real world, only in the mirror's world. I shook it. The lion woman head in the mirror didn't move.

She was more beautiful and strange than any human

woman I had ever seen, and she was sinister at the same time. But she was right: I was going to have to deal with stuff like this if I ever wanted to make it to the temples. "Do you know what happened?" I asked her. "About Lulu making that speech, and turning the whole school against me and—"

Didn't I tell you already? purred the head. *I know everything that ever did happen, and everything that ever will happen. And I find your sister's behavior repellent.*

I wanted it to be perturbed; I wanted it to implode to Arteria. "What are the kids going to do? Other kids got beat up at that school, really bad. Is that how I'm going to die? Why won't you tell me, if you know everything? When did you ever help me?" I dared to say, suddenly out of control myself because of how scared I was about school. The questions came pouring out. "What is it about the Time Temples? Will they really help me, or are you just luring me there into more danger? I don't believe you can take me to Arteria again, and I don't believe—"

I am very perturbed! roared the lion woman head, and the room went fuzzy.

Just in time I remembered to look at my watch. It was one-thirty P.M. exactly.

The room blacked out.

chapter 8

But I wasn't in Arteria, I was on Earth, standing outside the fence that surrounded the fire department's abandoned practice rescue tower. It was nothing but an old cast-iron fire escape, supported by a cement structure. Signs on the fence said DANGER and KEEP OUT.

I could also see myself at the foot of the tower, surrounded by a gang of tough eighth-graders. I didn't know how they had gotten me over the fence. But now I could hear them shouting at me to climb the tower, to prove I wasn't a baby, an embarrassment to the school.

The cold October weather was exactly like it was today. This could be happening tomorrow. Was this an event from the future, stored within the boltzmon, that it was showing me now?

I was too scared to stand up to the kids, too scared to

show them what a baby I was—even though I was terrified of heights. They didn't know that. If they had, it wouldn't have made any difference.

I started up the fire escape. The treads were just strips of metal; you could see right through them to the ground. And even though I was only watching myself climb higher and higher, just the sight of it made me feel dizzy and panicky.

It's not often I have the pleasure of feeling someone observe his own death, chuckled a voice inside my head. I saw then that the ash was in my gloved hand.

"Get me out of here!" I whispered fiercely.

And miss the show? Don't be ridiculous!

"When is this going to happen?"

It happened forty years ago. And it will happen again, if you don't get to the Time Temples—and if you fall into any traps when you are there. Be quiet. You're interrupting the show.

Lulu wasn't there. She must be at cheerleading. Most likely she didn't even know this was happening; and if she did, she would probably stop it before it got life-threatening. She was nasty; she wanted to humiliate me. But did she really want to put me in physical danger?

"But now that I know this happened, why can't I just not go here?"

If not this, they will make you do something else.

I was nearing the top of the tower on the old rusty

stairs. I could see myself trembling with terror, and I could not imagine how I could stand being up so high. But some of the kids were actually cheering me on now.

And then a step broke—the old cast-iron structure had rusted through. Down I plummeted, and just lay there in a broken heap.

The kids shouted. They hadn't wanted this to happen. Then they took off, suddenly silent, getting away fast before anyone could find them and blame them.

This happened forty years ago, the boltzmon reminded me. *And it will almost certainly happen again, because you are too stupid to know where we are. In fact, you are being* so *stupid that I am perturbed—perturbed to the breaking point.*

The staircase, and the pathetic crumpled figure beneath it, blinked away.

I was on the back steps of the immigration shed in Arteria. Ahead of me, beyond a flat wooden bridge over a rushing river, loomed the jungle, palm trees waving above the denser trees underneath. The leaves sighed. It was very dark under those trees.

I was still reeling from what I had just seen. The boltzmon said it had happened forty years ago. Did that mean it had happened on *this* version of Earth, which was forty years ahead of ours? Did it mean I had died at eleven on this planet, and that the blonde was Lulu at age fifty-three? I didn't know.

What I did know was that the boltzmon had not said my death would *definitely* happen that way again. It had said it would happen if I didn't get to the Time Temples or if I got caught in a trap there. That meant there was hope—if I got to the temples soon enough.

A rutted dirt track began at the bottom of the steps. A vehicle sat there, a wooden cart with two huge wheels supporting a square platform with a low railing around it. The wheels were so big they covered the length of the platform and rose several feet above the railing. Their roundness dominated the shape of the cart, giving the effect of a kind of bubble.

Harnessed to the cart was a large shaggy animal like a bull with sharp, curving horns.

The cart was beautiful in a way, because of its shape and because of the intricate carving on its railing and on its wooden wheels. There were no seats or benches. A young Arterian woman was already sitting in it on the floor; she was dressed all in white, holding a red umbrella over her head, shade against the glaring noonday sun. Awn and Sai were just climbing on. There was a break in the railing in front to make room for a little extension of the platform, and that's where the driver sat, a small, skinny boy wearing only a pair of filthy torn cutoffs. He looked as if he never got enough to eat. The reins in the boy's hands were attached by pins to the animal's nose.

Awn beckoned. "Hurry onto the *gwian* so we can get away from that terrible woman fast," he called to me. "I already paid a quarter of a *talay* for you."

"Thank you!" I called back. I had no money on me.

Which one was the boltzmon? Was it still the immigration inspector inside? Or was it the Arterian woman, or the driver? I wanted to find out as soon as possible.

I climbed onto the *gwian*. It was primitive but very well cared for. The wood was polished; the intricate carvings stood out in sharp relief. The animal was carefully groomed, his fur clean and brushed. The driver cared a lot about his animal and his *gwian*; they clearly meant more to him than just a means of earning money.

Both women had woven baskets. There was just enough room for the four of us seated on the floor behind the driver to spread out a little, but it wasn't comfortable. I tried to remember how far it was to the temples. My legs would be cramped and sore after a short time on this thing.

"Pai! Pai!" the driver called out in a singsong voice, and flicked the reins. The animal took a step forward. The wheels creaked. The *gwian* rocked on the rough track.

"Hey! Are you going to the bus? Wait for me!" brayed a gratingly familiar voice from behind us. My eyes met Awn's and Sai's, and I knew they had the same sinking feeling that I did. We turned to look. The *gwian* kept slowly rocking forward.

The blonde staggered ungracefully down the steps from the immigration shed, her large Prada bag slung over her shoulder. "Well, I finally got past that awful immigration man," she said. She grinned toothily, as though she thought we were her friends.

But her smile faded fast when she took in the *gwian*. "*This* is how we're supposed to get to the bus?" she said, frowning and stopping abruptly at the bottom of the steps.

"No! This is how we Arterians are going to the temples," Awn called out to her.

"My guidebook said they had air-conditioned buses!"

"They do! They do!" Awn said quickly. "One will be in front very soon. We take the *gwian* because we have so little money. Better for you to wait for the bus in front."

She stomped her foot and cursed, then hurried after us. "There *was* a bus, I know it, and it left already! *That's* where all those other people are. That stupid immigration man made me miss it, for no reason. I could kill him!"

"There will be another bus, very soon," Awn said eagerly. "You will not have to wait long."

She glared suspiciously at him, running after us with her bag. "How would you know, if you're too poor to take the bus?" she said, panting.

"We know that rich foreigners like you always take the bus," Sai said. "It is so much more comfortable, and for you not expensive. It takes the real jungle road, not the *gwian* track, so it is faster—and much, much safer."

"But how do I know the bus will really come?" the blonde objected, still chasing us. "That thing you're in is a piece of junk, for sure," she said insultingly. "But it's here, and I've got to get to the temples. And I'm tough." She lifted her chin as she ran, exposing her wattled neck.

The driver jerked the *gwian* to a halt, and the blonde got closer. "They have armed guards on the bus," the driver said in an unexpectedly mature voice for someone who looked so young. "The bus is safer for you. If the bandits see a foreigner with a bag like that, on the *gwian* track . . ." He slid a finger across his throat. "We are all poor Arterian people, and without you they may leave us alone. But if you are with us, we will all be in great danger. We cannot take you." He turned back and spoke to the animal and shook the reins. The *gwian* started forward again.

The blonde stood there for a moment, her chin jutting out in a way that was very familiar to me. I was more sure than ever now, crazy as it seemed, that this woman was Lulu as an adult.

She was so wrinkled and flabby that she didn't resemble the thirteen-year-old Lulu I knew. And I hadn't managed to see the name on her passport. But she sure acted like Lulu—even grown-up, she hadn't learned a thing about how to behave. If she *was* Lulu, I knew that the driver telling her she couldn't come with us would only make her more determined to ride the *gwian*. Endangering others didn't matter to her. Getting her own way did.

The blonde fumbled frantically in her bag. She pulled

out a fat paperback and thumbed through it. “Stop!” she bellowed. “My guidebook says the bus service from here is only once a day. I already missed it because of that horrible immigration man. It says the rumors of the bandits are exaggerated. I’m coming with you! I’ll pay you more than all those other people put together. Wait for me!”

I was scared of her. But I remembered how she had listened to me on the boat when I had been tough and insisted. And, Lulu or not, I didn’t want her coming with us. “If the bandit rumors are exaggerated, then why do they have armed guards on the bus?” I shouted at her. “It’s not worth risking your life for this.”

“The book doesn’t say anything about guards on the bus,” she argued. “He made it up.” She dropped the book into the bag and hurried after us again. The driver flicked the reins and the bull picked up speed, but the blonde was still faster. We had almost reached the bridge when she grabbed the *gwian* railing, gasping for breath. “Let me on this thing!” she demanded.

The driver looked around at her, his head held high. There was something almost noble about his manner, despite how young he was and his obvious poverty. “This is my *gwian*, madam, and my bull pulling it. Our passenger limit is four. Please go back.”

The blonde dropped her bag into the *gwian*, where it

landed heavily on Sai's lap, and began hoisting herself up over the railing. "Ten *talays*," she said, grunting. "Ten *talays* to take me to the temples. I bet that's more than you got from all four of these people."

"Push her off," the boy said. "For her, nothing less than one hundred *talays*." He turned back to the bull.

"That's highway robbery!" the blonde shouted, one leg on the moving *gwian*, the other hopping along on the ground, her fat thighs jiggling. There was plenty of meat there for the bandits.

"You will find out about robbery and other things when the bandits see you," the boy said, shaking the reins to make the bull go faster. "Push her off."

Awn and I crawled to the back of the *gwian*, and we each grabbed one of her hands to pry it off the railing. I enjoyed it.

She knew she couldn't fight off the two of us. "Okay, okay, you ugly jungle brat! I'll give you a hundred."

"Now," said the driver calmly.

The blonde sighed. She took her foot off the still moving *gwian* and almost fell. She straightened up and reached into her waist pouch and pulled out a wallet and ran around to the front and counted out money and gave it to the driver, cursing at him. Her hair was wet and drooping. The driver counted the money silently, pocketed it, then halted the *gwian*. The blonde climbed on.

Now we were more crowded and uncomfortable than before. We would also be very vulnerable to the bandits in the jungle. Why had the driver allowed her on even for one hundred *talays*? Maybe he was so poor that such an amount of money was worth the risk of being attacked.

I didn't understand why the boltzmon had done this. The boltzmon was the immigration inspector, or had been when the blonde was going through. If he had not delayed her, she would be on the bus, not riding the *gwian* and attracting the bandits to us. Why had the boltzmon put her on the *gwian*? As usual, its motivation made no sense at all.

What I did understand was how unbelievably selfish and pushy the blonde was, endangering all of us for what was probably a cosmetic whim. She was prematurely aged because of her own bad habits. She probably wanted to go to the Time Temples to get young again, like plastic surgery—Awn had said some foreigners went for that reason. That was more important to her than our lives.

She plumped her bag against the railing and leaned back against it. Because of the bag she was more comfortable than everyone else. No one spoke as we readjusted our legs, folding them underneath us more than before, to make room for her. She reclined with her legs outstretched. She probably believed she deserved to be more comfortable because she had paid so much more.

The *gwian* moved across the bridge, rocking on the rough planks, the wheels clacketing. The bridge had no railing. The rushing water below us was dark and foamy, its roar so loud that we would have had to scream to be heard. We could see the water through the missing planks on the bridge. The driver guided the *gwian* carefully around them. Twenty yards ahead, at the end of the bridge, the track entered a dark tunnel of green. The jungle.

I took a good look at the young Arterian woman for the first time, now that things were a little calmer. She was very beautiful, with full lips and big dark eyes. Her black hair was so long that it lay on the floor. She smiled at me. "Hello," she said, and moved her umbrella over so that it shaded me as well. "My name is Ayo."

"Er . . . I'm Chris," I said, feeling myself blushing. "I . . . I can hold that for you."

"Hold it over here," the blonde ordered me. "I'm hot on this thing."

We ignored her. "Thank you, but I can manage," Ayo said. "Chris. I never knew an Arterian with that name."

I shrugged, not knowing what to say. Was Ayo the boltzmon? Was it the driver?

The *gwian* swayed across the end of the bridge and under the dark tunnel of trees. Suddenly it seemed like night, even though outside it was midday. I looked back. The entrance to the jungle was a golden arched doorway diminishing behind us as we moved ahead into darkness.

It was hushed under the trees. Now there were strange birdcalls, and flutterings in the leaves, and then a distant barking howl. I was glad it was distant.

And, of course, the constant sound of water from the rivers of Arteria. We clattered softly over another bridge, almost invisible under the trees. I wondered if there were missing planks in this bridge, too.

Ayo folded up the umbrella and put it in her basket.

"How can you see where you're going? Isn't there any kind of light on this stupid thing?" the blonde complained in her ringing voice.

"Please," the driver said very softly. "Best to be quiet here, and not attract animals, or bandits, with your loud foreign speech. Light attracts creatures, too. I know the way. Please be quiet, for the safety of all."

"You act like you're in control here, but you're just the driver," the blonde argued, speaking hardly any softer. There was a flicker of flame and then the smell of smoke. Her cigarette glowed in the darkness as she took a heavy pull.

"Put that out now, and careful, too," the driver said firmly. "The odor of burning will attract much danger."

"You act like this is a jumbo jet and not a falling-apart piece of junk," she grumbled.

"You will do as Lep says," Ayo said, and there was an oddly compelling power in her quiet voice. "I have made this trip with him several times. He knows how to be safe—or as safe as we can be." Who was she, I wondered, that she spoke with such authority—and had made this trip before?

"Hmph!" the blonde said. But she didn't argue, and she stopped talking, and we could hear the hiss as she put out the cigarette with wet fingers. I hoped she was as scared as the rest of us.

Which one was the boltzmon? Would the boltzmon be able to protect us if we were attacked? Maybe—if it was around. But none of these people had given any indication of being the boltzmon, as had the old lady on the boat and the immigration inspector. None of them talked about being perturbed. Maybe it had deserted me. Were we on our own in this jungle with wild animals and cannibals?

We lurched along in the darkness for what seemed like hours, listening to the snuffling breath of the bull and crossing smaller bridges over splashing streams. An occasional tendril or branch scraped across my face. I shifted position whenever my folded legs started to ache.

How much time was going by at home? If the same amount of time was passing there, by now Mom and Dad would be seriously missing me. And what if we were attacked?

Maybe Ayo knew just how dangerous it was—she said she had already made this trip with Lep. I was shy about starting a conversation with her, but my fear gave me the guts to speak. "So, uh . . . you've done this trip before?" I whispered to her. "Did you have trouble?"

"Better not to talk about it," she whispered back. "We got through alive. That is as much as we can hope."

"Why are you going to the temples?" I asked her.

"I live at the temples. I had to go away for my brother's wedding. I hope we will get back. That horrible woman!" she added very softly in my ear. The meaning was clear: If we didn't make it, the blonde would be the reason.

Why, why had the boltzmon forced the blonde on us?

The howls were closer to the track now, and there were more of them.

A grating snoring sound began. It was the blonde, the only one in a comfortable enough position to fall asleep.

I was sitting toward the front, just behind the driver. "Will that noise she's making attract anything dangerous?" I asked him.

"It's better than when she talks," he whispered.

"How long does it take to get to the temples—I mean, if we don't have problems along the way."

"We will have problems," Lep, the driver, answered. "Always. But if we are lucky, we maybe get there by sunset tomorrow. With stopping time to let Bom-bom feed and rest."

Bom-bom had to be the bull. I hoped Lep would let it stop soon. I had to go to the toilet and stretch my aching legs. But Lep had such an air of command that I didn't like to make personal requests of him.

Instead I said, "Sai said there was a jungle *road*, the way the bus goes. Why don't we go that way? Wouldn't it be quicker, and safer?"

"It goes the long way around. It is easier for the bus, but for the *gwian* it would take much, much longer, more than a week. This track is a shortcut, too small for the bus, and the bridges not strong enough. And the bandits like the big road better, because the rich foreigners go that way."

That was hopeful. I shifted position again, wondering how long my legs could hold out.

"It is sunset outside," Lep said. "And here is the clearing where Bom-bom can eat and relax." The *gwian* halted abruptly. Lep hopped off, and I could hear the snapping of the harness being released. Ayo started to get off.

The blonde grunted, awakened by the *gwian* stopping. "Huh? Wha' happenin'," she said dopily—and loudly.

"Please, everyone, be very quiet," Lep instructed us in an urgent whisper. "You may get out and stretch and relieve yourselves. But do not wander from the path. Usually this place is safe from bandits. But anything can be hiding nearby. Big animals, and snakes, too."

Something wailed, closer to the track than any of the previous animal sounds. Did I really have to stretch my legs and go to the bathroom after all?

I did. I climbed off the *gwian*. A little pale, patchy light filtered through the trees here, and my eyes had adjusted enough so that I could see the others getting off. Bom-bom drank from a small stream that ran across the track.

I turned away from the others and took only two steps and relieved myself—I didn't even want to get near the edge of the track, which was wider than usual here.

I looked straight ahead of me, past the clearing, into the jungle. I could see a little of the underbrush and tree trunks in the irregular blotches of fading orange light. My eyes moved around. I finished and started to turn back.

And then I saw the big, hairy man, wearing a stained bandanna, crouched in the underbrush five feet in front of me.

A scorched human hand poked out of his shirt pocket, most of the flesh gnawed from the bones—a snack.

chapter 10

It happened fast.

The man leapt at me so quickly that I was on the ground with my arms pinned behind me before I could even start to run. My face was in the dirt, and it was too dark to see much anyway, but I heard shouts and screaming.

"Who do you think you are?" shrieked the blonde, and then her voice was abruptly cut off.

How many bandits were there? What kind of weapons did they have? Were they going to kill us right away?

And where was the boltzmon, now when I needed it more than ever?

Rough hands rapidly tied my feet together with scratchy rope; I choked against the powerful stench of a long-unwashed body and the burned human flesh it carried. The rope was jerked up and knotted around my wrists, still behind my back. My blood rang with panic; I was expecting a knife in my throat at any instant.

Hoarse grunting. "Fatso was right," said a deep, coarse voice. "Who'd expect little Lep with all his know-how to be dumb enough to carry such a juicy roast? I can taste the crispy skin already. And rich, too! Lep wouldn't have risked it if it didn't pay him a good price."

"A hundred in his pocket. We'll be kind and let him keep the four quarters from the others. We can afford to be generous. Get a look at the meat's bag."

I could now see out of the corner of my eye flickering lights that seemed very bright to me. The bandits weren't afraid to carry lanterns.

"A real Prada!" exclaimed a third voice. "Don't see those much on the temple route. This meat must be really stupid to bring it here."

"And we all know stupid foreign brains are tastier than smart Arterian ones," said still another voice, this one female. I heard a slurping sound, like a hand being wiped across her wet mouth. "We shall eat the brain alive for a special treat."

"One, two, three!" someone counted. There was a communal grunt, the sound of several people lifting something heavy, and then staggering footsteps.

"Whew! More fat than it looks like on this one. We'll feed well tonight."

Muffled sounds of protest; they had gagged the blonde.

"Ow! The thing got me in the eye! A fighter."

"This knife will teach it to behave."

The cry of pain was loud even through the gag.

"There'll be more of that if you don't calm down. We don't have to kill you before we cook you. Think about that, and show some respect."

I could hear slow, heavy footsteps in the underbrush. They must be carrying the blonde off into the jungle, and leaving the rest of us here, tied up but unharmed.

"Everybody okay?" Lep whispered. He spoke our names one by one, and we each answered yes.

For a moment all I felt was tremendous relief. The bandits had taken the obnoxious blonde and left us alone, free to go to the temples, and a lot safer now without her.

And then it hit me: What if she really *was* Lulu? I groaned aloud; I couldn't hold it in.

Lulu had tormented me for as long as I could remember. Even as an adult, she had developed no redeeming qualities at all. We were so much better off without her. I didn't even know for sure if this horrible woman really was my sister.

But if she was, could I just let the bandits carry her away and eat her, and not try to save her?

Maybe I *could* let them do it. Would *she* save *me*? I thought of her pep talk and its result.

"She's a package, this one!" one of the bandits complained. They were still easy to hear. The blonde and the bag were preventing them from making a quick getaway.

"Boltzmon?" I said. My voice sounded very small under the vast sighing of the trees, the birdcalls, the weird chittering jungle noises. "Is anybody the boltzmon? Please. I need you more than ever."

"Boltzmon," I heard Ayo whisper. "How do you—"

"Boltzmon? What are you talking about? No time for nonsense now," Lep said. "I have a good knife. When I get—uh!—out of these ropes, I can cut all of you loose."

My hope was gone. Lep wasn't the boltzmon. And I knew that being attacked by bandits and tied up would have perturbed the boltzmon to the point of implosion. It couldn't be any of these people. It had deserted me in this terrible situation.

Lulu had done so many nasty things to me. The blonde might not even be her. But if she *was* Lulu, and I let them kill her, I would bear the guilt for the rest of my life. I thought of the time, so long ago, when she had tried to hold me, and Mom had pulled me away from her. Maybe she *had* wanted to love me, and things just hadn't worked out.

I had never been so terrified. My throat was dry; my stomach was tighter than the knots around my wrists. But I managed to croak. "Could you please untie me first? I . . . I have to go try to save her, before they get too far away."

They argued with me all at once.

"You can't fight the bandits! They will kill you!"

"Now we are safe, without her."

"This is the best thing that could happen for us."

"But . . . she might be my sister," I said. "What if she was your sister?"

"Your sister?" Lep said, his voice at my ear, his knife sawing away at my ropes. "Are you crazy? She is old enough to be your grandmother. She can't be your sister."

How could I explain? "Lep, believe me. There are many strange things in the world," I said. "In Arteria, and in foreign worlds, too. I don't have time to tell you everything. But I'm not crazy. She might really be my sister." My legs were free now, and he moved on to my wrists. "If you had a sister, even one as horrible as she is—would you let the bandits take her and not do anything?"

"I did have a sister, once," Lep said softly as he cut away the last strand of rope around my wrist. "Until she went with me to the Time Temples."

"The temples? They really are dangerous, then?"

"Very dangerous. I did not do the right thing when I was there with her. That is why she died. But like you said, there is no time to explain."

He was telling me that even if we did make it to the Time Temples, as impossible as that seemed at this moment, I still wouldn't be safe.

I forced myself not to worry about that now, and sat up and looked around quickly. Off to the left, I could see the bright flickering lanterns the bandits were carrying. It wasn't too late to catch up with them.

And then what would I do?

Awn had gotten out of his ropes on his own. The bandits had assumed we wouldn't try to save the blonde and hadn't spent a lot of time tying us up. We quickly released Ayo and Sai, with the help of Lep's knife.

"Come on, let's get this over with," he said.

Lep jumped lightly onto Bom-bom's back, and patted the place behind him. "We will ride—the ground is very wet here because of all the streams. And Bom-bom is strong."

"You're coming *with* me?" I said, my heart lifting.

"I am responsible for my passengers, even if they are crazy," he said. "Climb up."

"But you can't!" I said, even as I was clambering up onto the animal's back, Lep grasping me under my arms to help pull me up. For someone so skinny, he was strong, and he got me up there. I stretched my legs apart on Bom-bom's wide back. I was still arguing with Lep. "It's not fair—to you or the others. This is my problem."

"I had a sister once. And I know some things about this tribe of bandits. I know where their camp is. Without me, you have no chance. With me, you have a one percent chance. Do not speak, or they will hear. They are making enough noise to cover Bom-bom's footsteps—he is quieter than a person."

More than anything, I didn't want Lep to get hurt. But I couldn't tell him that; he had told me not to speak.

Bom-bom plodded with a rolling gait; I had to hold on to Lep's waist to keep from slipping off. Lep and Bom-bom knew how to negotiate through the dense, wet under-brush—my legs were dangling in it and my sarong was already soaked.

We drew closer to the bandits' lights and voices.

"If this meat doesn't stop kicking and squirming, I will cut it again."

"Bash it on the head. Then it will be still."

"No!" said the woman hungrily. "This meat needs to suffer. It will be alive and wide awake when we cook it. It will be more delicious that way, too."

They made greasy snorting noises of anticipation, even as they struggled with the blonde. It was not a pleasant sound.

We weren't getting any closer to the bandits. Lep was keeping enough distance so that they wouldn't notice us.

We rolled on and on, Bom-bom carefully picking up each hoof and squelching it down softly. No more light was filtering through the trees. The lanterns were our only guides. I wondered how we would ever find our way back. I knew it would be a miracle if we had that problem.

I had to stretch my legs very wide on Bom-bom's broad back, and that was beginning to hurt a lot. Lep was smaller than me, but he had probably been riding this animal for his whole life. I wanted to ask him how much farther we had to go, but I didn't dare to speak.

How much time was going by back at home? If it was the same as here, the police would be looking for me by now.

"Listen!" one of the bandits said suddenly. "Do you hear something behind us? Footsteps?"

"Go faster. The tigers are hunting tonight."

"I don't smell a tiger," the first bandit said. "I smell a clean animal. An animal I smelled before."

Lep murmured something, and Bom-bom stopped walking.

"You don't know what clean means," the woman said angrily. "It's all your imagination. Just keep going. Fatso will be getting impatient. He sent us out there, and he will want to see what we caught."

They began moving again, and so did we. I listened uncomfortably to the howling and yapping, not very far away. Would the wild animals be more attracted to the bandits, or to Bom-bom? At least Bom-bom was clean and didn't smell as much as the bandits.

Finally I began to be aware of a reddish glow in the distance. It was a large bonfire—the bandits' camp. The fire burning there meant there were more bandits waiting at the camp. How did Lep think we were going to get the blonde away from all those people? I had no idea in the world.

We should just turn back. The blonde probably wasn't Lulu. We were going to die for the sake of this horrible stranger. And even if she was Lulu, it was because of her that my life was in danger back at home.

Lep whispered "*Yute*" into Bom-bom's ear, and we stopped about twenty feet from the fire.

The group of bandits were shadows against it as they lurched into the clearing. There seemed to be four people struggling with the blonde, and another carrying her bag. Coarse voices shouted greetings, and then exclamations of excitement at what they had brought with them.

Lep took the opportunity to whisper to me, "This camp is closer to the road the buses take than to our track. They usually hide by that road, to attack the buses with rich foreigners. Bad luck they were waiting by the *gwian* track today. I have been thinking about that. I don't understand why they were there. Very strange. Almost like they knew I would have something special on this trip."

Almost like they knew. Yes, that was a strange kind of bad luck. Besides those of us in the *gwian*, who else knew the blonde was riding with us?

Only the boltzmon.

"Bring the meat and the plunder to me!" cried a loud guttural voice. "And stop screaming like noisy brats!"

The shouting subsided. Because of the firelight, I could get a good look at the bandits for the first time. A lot of them wore strange baggy shorts and bandannas, and most of the men had long hair and beards.

To the right of the fire was a kind of tent, vague in the shadows. In front of the tent, in a bamboo chair, sat a very fat man with a beard, wearing a stocking cap with a pom-pom on his bald head. He wasn't wearing a shirt, and his huge body hung from him in soft, sagging folds. A bottle sat by his side. A guard with a spear stood on his left, another on his right. The bandits dropped the struggling blonde in front of him, then set her Prada bag on his lap.

The blonde's wrists and ankles were tied, and another rope connected them, so that she was bent backward like a bow. She was also gagged with a thick rag. It must have been very uncomfortable. But that didn't stop her from thrashing angrily on the ground. She was a fighter, I had to give her credit for that. So was Lulu.

"The meat is bothering me with its pointless wormy squirming," said the fat man in the chair. "Make it stop."

"We want to keep it conscious and alive for the cooking," said the female, bowing to the chief.

"Then stand on it or something. I want to go through its bag without distraction."

The female bandit slammed her big booted foot onto the blonde's lower back. The blonde howled in pain through her gag, but she did lie still.

"Garbage . . . more garbage," the chief was saying, tossing what looked like cosmetics out of the Prada bag. "A bore!" He held the bag upside down and shook its contents out onto the ground in front of him, some of the stuff falling on the blonde—clothes and toiletries and cartons of cigarettes. "Is this all?" the chief said angrily.

"It is a Prada," someone said.

"What do I care?" the chief asked. "That name is of no value here."

"But it shows she is rich."

"We will be feasting," the woman bandit said. "And there is this, too." She handed him the blonde's waist pack.

"Ah, yes. Foreigners carry the important stuff in these stupid things," said the chief. He ripped open the pink bag and pawed through its contents. And then he murmured under his breath, as though he were counting.

He looked up, a broad grin spreading across his piggish features. He slipped a wallet into his pants pocket. "A foreign passport, always useful. Credit cards, useful if anyone goes to the city. And also . . ." He shrugged, then looked at his guards. He was still smiling. "Well, a few *talays* in cash," he said. Clearly it had to be a *lot* of *talays*, or he wouldn't have been grinning like he was. But he didn't trust the others enough to tell them how much. "What did I tell you?" he cried out, his voice grating and cracked with excitement. "Wait by the clearing on the *gwian* track at sundown, and we will be rewarded. We can feast!"

There was enough noise so that Lep could whisper, "If we are going to try to save her, it has to be now."

I felt like I was going to throw up. "But . . . but how? There are so many of them, and only two of us."

He shrugged sadly. "We get Bom-bom running fast and rush through there and grab her when they are not expecting it. It will be easier if she is still tied up."

I felt like crying, for Lep's courage and goodness. He knew it was hopeless, and we would probably die. And he was going to try it anyway. Why was he doing this for me?

The bandits dragged the blonde closer to the fire.

"We go now, before the cooking starts," Lep said.

"No, Lep," I said. "Don't. You brought me to the camp. That's enough. There's no reason for you and Bom-bom to die, for that horrible woman who only *might* be my sister. I'll go alone."

He sat up straight. "I will not let you go alone. I protect my passengers. I have a reputation. *Pai*," he whispered to

Bom-bom, in a different voice, and slapped him hard on the shoulder.

I almost tumbled off, Bom-bom took off so fast. I clung to Lep as Bom-bom raced toward the fire, directly for the blonde. We neared the clearing. They were hoisting her up onto a kind of bamboo grill. Her clothes were scorching.

We burst into the clearing. Bandits shouted and let go of the blonde. Lep bent way over and grabbed her by the rope, and I did, too. We dragged her off the grill.

But she was too heavy for us to carry, each with one arm only. We didn't let go. We slid off Bom-bom, right on top of her. Bom-bom was between us and the bandit chief, but in an instant the bandits had pulled him aside and surrounded us, knives at our throats. We stood there in front of the fat man in the chair.

"What is this outrage? How do you dare to break into my camp and try to steal my food?" bellowed the chief. "This is *very* perturbing!"

And then it all fell into place. As usual, I didn't understand *why* the boltzmon had done this. But at least I knew who the boltzmon was, finally.

"Why did you do this?" I shouted angrily at the bandit chief, the boltzmon. "You made her miss the bus so she'd have to ride the *gwian*; then you told the bandits where they could find her. You made it so we got attacked, and they took her, and Lep and I had to risk our lives to save her. Why?"

Lep was staring at me, wide-eyed, his mouth open. The bandits were glancing at one another fearfully. The guards stepped forward. No one ever spoke like this to the chief.

The boltzmon's hairy nostrils flared. "How dare you talk to me like that, little boy? I do what I want! You are perturbing me to the breaking point!"

I stamped my foot, imitating Lulu. "Well then, *get* perturbed! And while you're at it, be sure to get Lep and the blonde out of here safely—Lep first, if you have a choice."

His face was swelling up, getting bigger and bigger and redder and redder. *"I AM PERTURBED!"* he roared.

The world trembled and went black.

chapter 11

Back in my room again, no ash in my hand.

Where was the boltzmon?

My heart was thudding, I was gasping and dripping with sweat. But I did remember to look at the desk clock. It was one-thirty when I left. Now it was ten o'clock.

We had left the immigration shed in Arteria around noon, and it was nine P.M. when we attacked the bandits' camp. Nine hours had gone by in Arteria, and nine hours here. Maybe time went at the same rate in both places, but now I knew it didn't matter, because the boltzmon could bring me back to whatever moment it felt like. That paper I found on the Internet said it had the ability to warp space and time, like a black hole. Warping space was how it could send me back here without coming itself.

If it wanted, it could bring me at any instant to the moment of my death—and not as an observer.

I shivered and pushed that thought out of my mind. It was going to be tough to explain to Mom and Dad where I had been until ten P.M., and why I hadn't phoned.

And where was the boltzmon? Had it left me for good? What was happening to Lep and the blonde?

"Maybe in his e-mail address book," Mom said in the hallway, and burst into the room, looking distraught. "Chris!" she cried out, her eyes widening. She hugged me impulsively, then backed away. "Where were you? Why didn't you call? And where's Lulu?"

I felt a pang. "Lulu's not here?" I said.

"No! And neither were you, until this minute. Why did you sneak into the house and up here without telling us?" Now she was angry. "Where's Lulu?" she said. "Dad's been calling her friends, and I've been calling yours."

"Lulu's not here?" I said again, stupidly, imagining all sorts of horrible things.

"You don't have any idea where she is?"

"No," I said. Maybe she was in Arteria. Maybe she was in some other weird universe. Maybe she was hanging out with her friends. I didn't know. But I was pretty sure the boltzmon had a hand in whatever had happened to her.

Dad rushed in. "Chris! Where is she?" he said, as if my return didn't mean anything and only Lulu mattered.

"I don't know."

"Where were you?" Mom said. "Why didn't you call?"

"I . . . I took a walk."

"You expect us to buy that?" Mom said.

"I was thinking about Arteria," I said.

"Arteria? What's Arteria?" Mom said.

"This isn't helping us find Lulu," Dad said abruptly, not interested. But at least it got me off the hook.

"You called her friends?" I said.

"The last time anybody saw her was when she left cheerleading practice at four-thirty," Mom said. "We've called everybody we can think of." She turned to Dad. "We'd better call the police," she said in a hollow voice.

Dad looked ashen. He left the room silently.

"You can make yourself a sandwich if you're hungry," Mom said. "I want to hear what the police have to say."

I sat down on the bed and thought hard. Why had the boltzmon sent me back here and not itself? Had it stayed back there, disguised as the bandit chief, to deal with Lep and the blonde? I hoped so. How long would that take? I looked at my watch. I had been back for twenty minutes now.

I thought of something and took the old pair of running shoes out of my closet. They were empty. I felt hopeless. Had it done something to Lulu and then deserted me for good?

And then, suddenly, the ash appeared in the left shoe. *Leave me alone.*

I quickly put back the shoes and sank down on the bed again in relief. I wanted the boltzmon to tell me what was going on, and where Lulu was. But I knew now that it didn't answer questions in this mood. Somehow, I felt more and more strongly that Lulu was in Arteria. And if she was there, then I had to go back fast. I could perturb the boltzmon and hope it would implode me back there.

But I couldn't do it now. Mom and Dad would notice I was missing. I had to eat something and then pretend to go to bed. If they believed I was asleep, they might leave me alone—they would be preoccupied about Lulu. And *then* I could try to get the boltzmon to help me find her.

An hour later, at eleven P.M., Mom and Dad were pacing and drinking coffee. Some cops had come and gotten Lulu's picture, and they were cruising around looking for her and questioning people. I said good night to Mom and Dad. Mom hugged me and said she was glad I was home. Dad was so worried about Lulu he barely noticed.

The strange thing was that I cared, too. I was really worried about Lulu. For some reason I loved her. It had taken this situation to make me realize that. I remembered the times in the past when she had reached out to me. There must have been other good times, too. They had been blotted out of my conscious mind by all the bad memories, and I couldn't pinpoint them exactly. But now I knew they were there. And I was determined to find her.

I had been up for much longer than a normal day, but I hardly felt tired at all. I got the boltzmon out of the shoe. It still looked like a little gray ash.

Leave me alone. I'm still upset.

"I have to find Lulu. What did you do with her?"

I don't feel like talking about it.

"Well, I do. I feel like talking about a lot of things. Is the blond woman Lulu as a grown-up? Why did you fix it so the bandits captured her, and Lep and I had to go and save her? We could have died! And now Lulu's gone anyway. Are you trying to kill me, and Lulu, too? Is *that* why you inflicted yourself on me?"

I don't like the word inflict. *Nor do I care for your tone of voice.*

"Look. *You* put us in this terrible situation. Mom and Dad are going nuts. Do something!"

I play by my own rules.

"So are you going to let whatever horrible mess Lulu's in just keep going on? Or are you going to help me find her? Do you know where she is?"

This is very boring. Of course I know where she is. I flipped her over to the Time Temples, that's all.

I groaned. Lep said his sister had died because of going

there. "She'll have no idea where she is. I've got to get there and help her."

Very pushy fellow, aren't you? When people are too pushy, it makes me very irritable.

I was finally getting somewhere. "Well then, *be* irritable, jerk! I'm finding out that I'm tough and I can do things I never thought I could. But it's still your fault I'm in this mess. If you're not a monster, you'll put me in a place where I can save Lulu and help Lep."

I squeezed the ash between my fingers and shook it.

Hey! I don't like that. That hurts!

"Then get perturbed and get me out of here!"

I'm perturbed, all right! And I'll get you out of here. Here we goooooooo!

The room fizzled and went black. A second later I opened my eyes.

I screamed.

This wasn't Arteria.

chapter 12

My shoes were sinking down into a pinkish, spongelike foam. Blood vessels pulsed through it—it was a living organism. Other organisms, like red worms, zipped curiously around my ankles now as I sank. The air was thin, hard to breathe. I was gasping.

I wasn't in Arteria, I was in some other, much more bizarre and hostile world. Was the boltzmon even around to get me out of here?

"Help!" I weakly called out. My voice was squeaky and high-pitched, like a cartoon character's voice. "Please! Take me away from here!"

The stuff was now around my knees. I was sure it was going to start digesting me any minute. I struggled to get my feet out, but the stuff clung to me. And the gravity must be stronger here. I felt heavy, and it was hard to move.

The stuff began to ripple as I sank, the foam moving up above my waist now. The ripples were made by a large creature wriggling toward me, a thing like a jellyfish, transparent, with slimy organs inside it. Its long tentacles pulled it through the foam. It had a wicked beak.

"Boltzmon, please! Why did you do this? Please, I'll . . ." But I was too out of breath to say any more.

The jellyfish ate several of the little red worms. I could see them sinking down into its transparent body, and the organs inside beginning to digest them. Maybe I was too big for it to eat! But that didn't mean it couldn't take bites out of me. There was no way I could run away from it.

I looked around frantically for the boltzmon. The sky was green. In the distance I saw land, rocks, squat bulbous buildings. Not that I could get anywhere near them before the foam or the jellyfish got to me.

The foam was now up to my chest, the jellyfish tentacles only a few feet away. "Boltzmon!" I managed to gasp. "Please . . ."

There was no answer. It wasn't here. It had been *so* perturbed that it lost control and imploded me to this place. I couldn't depend on it always to take me to Arteria, like it had done the other times. The boltzmon was not something you could *ever* depend on, for anything.

I squirmed away from a jellyfish tentacle. It reached out

and touched my neck. It felt like an electric shock. With what little breath I had, I screamed.

The red worms were still writhing around me. One of them stopped in front of my face—the sponge had reached my shoulders. *You've developed the bad habit of taking me for granted,* said the worm.

"Boltzmon!" I cried out, overjoyed. "Hurry, get me out of here."

Did you hear what I said?

"Taking you for granted?" I said, trying to think, to ignore the other stinging jellyfish tentacle on my cheek. And even in this situation, I couldn't help feeling irritated by the boltzmon. "Is it taking you for granted for me to go and try to save that blond woman, with no help from you?" I demanded, with what felt like my last breath.

Yes, you did win that one. But the others will not be so easy. And so I will relent and answer some of your questions.

Now, when I was about to be eaten by a monster jellyfish, it had decided to answer my questions? But it might be my only chance. "Okay, hurry, answer!"

As a black hole in the future, I absorbed your solar system and also the solar system containing the Earth-like planet with Arteria on it. The planet is part of me, as is the DNA of all the creatures on it. To pinpoint their DNA, warp them out of the way and take their forms, to warp people from your world to there and back, is as simple to me as breath-

ing is to you. I still possess the time- and space-warping powers of the black hole I was.

"But why does everything have to be so difficult, then?" I persisted, my mouth just above the foam. "Why can't you just bring Lulu back so Mom and Dad won't miss her? Why can't you fix it yourself so that I'm not going to die so soon, so I don't have to go to the Time Temples? Why can't you make it so Lulu doesn't hate me? Why can't you—"

I am an astronomical object, not your own private genie! There are limits to what I can do. I can go between the planets I absorbed and send people between them as well, and I can take many forms on certain planets. And that's it. The rest is up to you. And that is why you must experience the dangers and trials of the Time Temples, in order to—

And then a jellyfish tentacle grabbed the worm, pulling it toward its beak.

Stop that! You are perturbing me! cried the worm.

And just as my mouth sank into the foam, the world fizzled and went black.

Back in the darkness of the jungle on the *gwian* track. I groaned with relief. The jungle was scary, but better than where I had just been.

My eyes gradually adjusted. I was in the same clearing where the bandits had attacked. Afternoon light filtered through the trees. Was it the next day? I hoped the *gwian* was ahead of me. I took a moment to catch my breath, then hurried along the track.

The track sloped uphill now, with sharp turns in it, switchbacks. I couldn't go very fast, climbing.

From the small clearing at the top of the hill I saw that there was a valley ahead, tops of trees everywhere, and then another higher hill beyond it—the mountains. I heard the sounds of waterfalls.

I peered down the descending track. I could see a little

movement in the darkness ahead, a bubblelike roundness. Was it the *gwian*? Now, going downhill, I ran.

They did not cry out when they saw me. They were still keeping quiet, even though other bandits did not seem to be bothering them now.

Bom-bom stopped, and the *gwian* rolled forward a little on the hillside. They were all beaming at me and saying how happy they were to see me. Only the blonde was frowning, and silent for a change.

"Come. We have to hurry to make up for the time we lost. And the road ahead is hard," Lep said. I got into the *gwian*, and we started off again. It took me a long time to get my breath back. The *gwian* was slow, but still faster than normal walking pace, especially in the hills.

Finally, after many minutes had gone by, I said, "What happened to you back at the bandit camp?"

"You are shouting orders at the bandit chief," Lep said, shaking his head in wonderment. "Telling him to get the two of us out of there. And then the bandit chief screamed, and you weren't there."

"Poof!" muttered the blonde irritably. "Can't wait to hear you try to explain *that* little trick."

What was the matter with her *now*? We saved her life, didn't we?

"So then what happened?" I asked.

"Very strange," said Lep. "The bandit chief shouted at them to let us go. He said he had all the important stuff, I was too skinny to eat, and the foreign meat would make them sick, he knew by the smell. The bandits have to follow their chief. We rode back. I let Bom-bom have a long rest before starting into the mountains."

That's why the boltzmon had come back to my room later than me; it had stayed in the form of the bandit chief long enough to let them go.

We rolled down to the bottom of the valley, crossed a rough bridge over a loud foaming river, and started up the next dark switchback.

The blonde was wearing long baggy shorts and an oversized T-shirt, both filthy. "So the bandits gave you some clothes to replace the scorched ones?" I asked her.

"They're so gross and smelly they make my skin crawl," she complained. "They gave me back my Prada bag, but they didn't give me my wallet, my money, my credit cards, my passport. How am I going to manage at the temples? How am I ever going to get home?"

I was angry, and now I wasn't afraid to show it. "You didn't mention the little fact of your *life*," I said. "If it weren't for Lep and me, you'd be a pile of bones now."

She shrugged. "Thanks," she said, in a voice so dull and perfunctory it was like a slap in the face.

I opened my mouth to shout at her.

"Ignore her," Lep said. "She's been that way ever since we left the camp. Don't pay any attention."

"So what happened to *you?*" the blonde wanted to know, eyeing me strangely. "How did you just pop out of existence like that? If you can do that, I bet you can do other things that might be a little more helpful to me."

"What could be more helpful than saving your life?"

"Don't change the subject. How did you do that?"

The other times I had vanished, on the boat and in the immigration shed, she must have been too preoccupied to notice. The others were all watching me, curious, too. I had to come up with something.

"Sometimes it just happens. I suddenly go to another place." I glanced at the blonde. "Maybe more like the country you come from. But I can't control it. And I can't bring anybody with me, either." I shrugged. "When it happens, it happens, and I can't do anything about it."

"Yeah. Sure," the blonde said.

"If I could control it, I'd have done it when the bandits first attacked, instead of waiting, right?"

"Yes. That makes sense," Lep said as we labored up the hill, the *gwian* creaking past the sound of a rushing stream in the darkness. "But it still means you are some kind of . . . wizard."

"No, I'm not. I can't make it happen. I'm just a kid who fell into this. Believe me." I didn't want any of them to start thinking I could do magic or anything.

"Well, we are glad to have you back, safe," Ayo said, smiling at me—I could just make out her white teeth. "And you and Lep are very brave for what you did. We will be late, but we may make it to the temples after all."

"Yeah, and what good will it do *me* to get there, without any money or anything else," the blonde said.

"I told you many times already," Ayo said imperiously. "The temples are not about money! What you find there, what changes there, depends on your heart."

"There's no such thing as a free lunch," the blonde said, contradicting someone who knew more about the temples than she ever would. "There's no place in the world where money doesn't mean something. Thirteen thousand *talays* they stole from me!" She seemed to care more about her money than her own life. "Why don't you just pop back there to the camp and get some of it back for me," she said to me sarcastically.

"I told you, I can't control it!" I said.

"Quiet," Lep said softly. "We don't talk now."

We passed the next hour silently. Finally the *gwian* moved around the last switchback, nearing the top of the hill now. Beyond it blazed a brightness that dazzled my eyes. There was sky beyond the crest, open sky not hidden by trees.

We reached the top, and the *gwian* stopped. Lep and Ayo were the only ones who didn't gasp.

The track ended at the edge of a cliff. Nine hundred thirty-seven feet below roared a river almost as big as the Aortazon, a fury of white-capped waves and rapids and water smashing against stone. The river was wide, the cliff on the other side 310 feet away.

And in the distance on the other side, outlined by the glow of the huge red sun, rose tall, glittering minarets. It was hard to tell how many, or to discern their exact design. To see them was to crave to go to them.

"The Time Temples," Ayo whispered.

And that was where Lulu was, the real, thirteen-year-old Lulu—heavily made-up, in her cheerleading outfit. What was happening to her there? How dangerous was it? Lep had said his sister had died because of going there. Would we get there in time?

I knew there was some kind of bridge across this tremendous chasm, to the right of the track. I turned and looked.

I shuddered, and my stomach knotted. It was a rope bridge with a wood plank floor, 310 feet long, drooping in the middle, dangling 937 feet above the wild river. I had thought this bridge was so exciting when I put it onto the computer map. Now I had to cross it. And I was terrified of heights.

It swayed in the wind.

Lep shaded his eyes with his hand. "I think we can make it before it gets too dark," he said. "But we must start right away. We don't want to be on the bridge when night falls. Bom-bom would be scared, and unpredictable."

"Er . . . maybe we could camp here and get an early start in the morning," I suggested.

"I must get back as soon as possible. We are late already, and I have missed so many of my duties," Ayo said, touching my hand, pleading with her big dark eyes. She smiled at me. "The bridge is strong, and it doesn't take long. You will see."

"We must go now," said Sai, and Awn nodded.

"You think you're going to get me on that . . ." the blonde started to say. Her voice faded. She was gazing at the temples, sparkling in the orange sunlight. "Yeah. Maybe we do need to go."

Now I felt the pull of the temples, too. As much as I hated heights, I knew I had to get there. If I didn't, I would die. I had seen it with my own eyes.

Lep maneuvered Bom-bom to the bridge. Daintily, Bom-bom set his hooves onto the wooden planks. He stepped out over the chasm. Lep stroked his flank, comforting him.

The *gwian* clattered here as never before; the plank bridge flooring was tied in place, and the boards shifted when the wheels bore down on them. Three strands of thick rope stretched on either side, the top one at the level of the gwian railing. The bridge swayed every time Bom-bom took a step. He did not go quickly.

I looked down at the cascading river, so very far below us. I felt sick on the tilting bridge. I looked back up at the temples. They calmed my stomach. I had to get there. I stared at them, trying to forget about the bridge.

It didn't help that the bridge was sloping downward now. I turned back to see how far we had come. Only a quarter of the way across.

Lep kept stroking Bom-bom. Ayo sat placidly beside me, her face glowing as she gazed at the temples. Awn clutched his mother's hand in both of his. The blonde clung tensely to the railing. I realized I was doing that, too.

We reached the very lowest point of the bridge and started up, swinging back and forth. Maybe we really were going to make it across.

"No," Lep said suddenly, in a voice more frightened than when we had been at the bandit camp.

Another *gwian*, pulled by an animal like Bom-bom, was just stepping out onto the other end of the bridge.

"But why isn't he waiting for us to cross?" I said.

"He is wrong," Lep said.

"The bridge isn't wide enough for both! Is it even strong enough to carry two *gwians?*"

"No," Lep said. "It is the rule not to go onto the bridge if there is someone else on it first." He shook his head. "I don't understand. I know that driver. He would never do this."

The wind tossed my hair, whistling in the chasm. The sun was sinking fast now. What would Bom-bom do if we were still on the bridge when it got dark?

"But we're halfway across already," the blonde said, sitting up straight, full of righteous indignation. "That driver *has* to wait until we get off before he gets on."

"That is the rule," Lep said, stroking Bom-bom nervously. "This driver must have gone crazy. I don't know what to do. If I leave Bom-bom he will spook." I had never heard Lep sound so disheartened.

Beside me Ayo's head was bowed, her eyes closed, her hands pressed together against her forehead. Was she praying? That made it only scarier. Could we possibly get past the other *gwian* without falling?

Lep waved his arm at the other driver to go back.

The driver made the same gesture back at Lep.

"What is he, some kind of *moron?*" the blonde said, in her most irritating, bossy voice. "We were here first! He can't get away with this!"

A few minutes ago she had been clutching in fear at the

gwian railing. Now she climbed off the *gwian* as if we were on a regular road and not dangling 937 feet up. She grabbed onto the top bridge rope with her right hand and stomped past the *gwian*, rocking the bridge even more.

"She is a terrible woman, and has made a lot of trouble," Awn murmured. "But maybe she can help now."

"That driver has gone crazy," Lep said, and then added dryly, "but he doesn't know what she is like."

The blonde teetered along the bridge ahead of us, her back bent slightly forward, her gait resolute and determined. Just the way Lulu was when she felt somebody was infringing on her territory, real or imagined. Lulu, forty years older on this world than the Lulu on our world.

I had to give her credit. I was too scared to get out of the *gwian*. Everyone was too scared, except Lep, and he had to stay with Bom-bom. But not the blonde.

She was lighter than Bom-bom and not pulling a *gwian*, so she went faster, though we kept moving, too. The other driver was watching her now. He was middle-aged, with a hawklike face. His passengers sat in shadow.

The blonde waved at him. We were close enough now so that we could just barely hear her voice over the water. "Get back there! Now! That's the rule. We were on the bridge first! Do you want to kill everybody?"

The driver ignored her, lifting his chin, and shook the

reins. His *gwian* was in bad repair, missing rungs on the railing and spokes on the wheels; his animal's fur was not sleek like Bom-bom's, its skin bare in places.

"You can't ignore me!" the blonde shouted. She had reached him now. She planted herself directly in front of his animal and held out her arm, palm up. "Go back!"

"Get out of my way, you stupid foreigner." He lifted a whip from the seat beside him. Lep didn't have a whip.

"You want me to spook your animal?" screamed the blonde. "I'll spook it all right. And then you'll all go over the edge."

"Please. She is right. Go back," came a chorus of voices from the passengers.

"Be quiet!" he told them. "We have to get across before sunset."

One of the passengers stood up. "The foreigner is right. We will walk back. Give us our money now."

"Why do you listen to a foreigner who knows nothing?"

"She speaks the truth!" One by one, his passengers were climbing off. This driver had squeezed eight people into a *gwian* that was the same size as Lep's and meant to carry only four. More work for the animal, more dangerous and uncomfortable for the passengers, more money for the driver.

The passengers stood in line on one side of his *gwian*,

each holding out a hand for the money, clinging to the rope with the other, barely managing to stand. The bridge was tilting more in the wind now.

The driver swore and lifted his whip at the blonde.

She didn't flinch. She put her hand on the animal's rein, right where the pin pierced its nose. The animal whinnied uncomfortably.

We had stopped now, too close to move any farther ahead. The sun was very near the horizon. This had to be resolved fast, or the animals would freak on the bridge in the darkness.

The driver lifted his fist and shook it. Then he leaned forward and said something to his animal. It took one step backward, then another.

The blonde had won. She had saved us all.

chapter 14

The sun was below the horizon when we finally reached the end of the bridge, but it was not yet completely dark.

The blonde came back and rode the rest of the way with us. We all congratulated and thanked her for what she had done. She tried to act indifferent to it, but I recognized the smug look in her eye. I was more sure than ever that she *had* to be Lulu as an adult.

What would that mean at the Time Temples, the two of them there together?

The other driver was standing beside his animal a few yards from the bridge, blocking the road, his passengers clustered behind. "Thank you, Lep, with your shiny *gwian* and healthy young animal," the driver said sarcastically. "Now I have to wait all night before going across. And this . . . this *foreigner* of yours has turned my passengers away. Do you think I'm going to let you pass?"

"Why are you acting so strangely?" Lep asked. "You know the bridge rule."

"Don't perturb me with your stupid little rules!" the driver snarled.

Then I knew what the driver really was. I wanted to get away from him before he got *too* perturbed.

"Let us pass, please," Lep said calmly. "We have a ways to go before we can rest."

The driver moved closer, lifting his whip. "Your animal is pampered. It doesn't understand discipline."

"You touch Bom-bom, and I'll kill you with my bare hands," Lep said, his voice scary because his tone was so matter-of-fact.

A tall and heavily built young man stepped forward. "Let them pass," he said, "or the eight of us you cheated will all together push you over the cliff."

The other passengers muttered in agreement.

The driver turned back to them in surprise. He could tell—as I could—that their threat was real. The driver's head and neck sank forward. He looked vile and defeated, like a vulture deprived of his prey. He glared balefully at Lep. "This is very disturbing," he said. Then he pulled his animal to the side, making the road clear for us. We rolled quickly past him. To my great relief he was only disturbed, not perturbed enough to implode.

"Not a good enemy to have, that driver," Lep murmured. He shrugged. "But I have no choice. He was crazy today."

Why had the boltzmon purposely made trouble for us on the bridge? Its motivation still made no sense to me.

In the last fading light I could see that the road, which twisted and turned along the edge of the chasm, was very different from the jungle road. The ground was exposed stone here, and the road was nothing but two wide uneven ruts in the stone. This road had not been built. It had been carved by the wheels of all the vehicles that had traveled this route. It must have taken many centuries.

All we could see of the temples now were narrow silhouettes against the emerging stars. Still, they pulled at me. Lep felt the pull, too, because he kept going for at least another hour through the night.

We crossed many streams, as always in Arteria. Here they plunged over the edge of the chasm, any one of the waterfalls dramatic enough to make a national park back at home. At last we came to one where Lep turned the *gwian* aside, to the right, away from the edge and onto soft earth where a few trees grew. "We will rest here," he said.

The Arterian women had little baskets of food, which they shared with everyone. It was simple food, grain and vegetables; we ate with our hands. It was delicious. The blonde, unexpectedly, thanked them when I did. She had been unusually quiet since the incident on the bridge.

We lay down on moss under the trees. I had no blanket and no pillow, but I had been awake for so long that I fell instantly asleep. I didn't open my eyes until I felt a hand on my shoulder, and looked up to see Lep's face in the dawn light. "Time to get to the temples," he said. We washed in the stream and started off, the sun rising behind us.

We were entering more civilized territory now. There was a sturdy wall along the edge of the chasm, the stones neatly and squarely cut. Trees and bushes and beds of flowers blossomed on the other side of the road.

We turned a sharp corner, and the temples loomed straight ahead of us, across a stream at the end of a long green field. The sight of them made me feel as though I were falling forward, and I grabbed at the *gwian* railing.

The temples shimmered with tiny reflecting stones of all colors. There was a large central tower like a narrow pyramid. Four smaller towers stood away from each of its corners. One of the smaller towers was inside a wall, with trees around it. Wide at the base, the temples tapered up into thin spires hundreds of feet high. The central tower was a series of square balconies connected by steep stairways, each balcony smaller than the one below, heavily carved with creatures that looked like demons.

Tourists, Arterians and foreigners, swarmed up and down the steps of the main temple and filled the balconies, taking pictures. But the side of the temple that was inside the wall was empty of people. Monstrous statues lined the edges of the crowded field leading to the towers. On both sides of the field were parking lots—on the left, a big, crowded paved one for buses, on the right, a small dirt one for the few *gwians*. There were indications of other buildings behind the temples, but it was the temples that held your eye.

"How come there're so many tourists if it's so dangerous to get here?" I asked.

"They don't all come from the river and the jungle like we did," Lep said. "The other routes are safer."

"It looks like the *gwian* track leads right to the front of the temples, the main entrance," I said with curiosity. "The buses come by the back way?"

Lep nodded. "The *gwian* track is the important route, the ancient route. Foreigners don't know that."

"Would you like a cold drink, sirs and madams?" piped a little voice.

A small ragged girl about seven years old stood beside the *gwian*. She held a tin bucket of ice with small bottles of drinks in it. "No, thank you," we all said, though if I'd had any money I would have bought something from her, just because she looked so poor and her smile was so pretty. We turned right, toward the *gwian* parking lot.

People wandered in the central field, tourists and Arterians. Strolling musicians tooted on pipes and sawed at one-stringed instruments and jangled bells, strange rhythmic music, joyous but with an edge of loss to it. Stalls shaded by big umbrellas sold food and drinks and trinkets and clothes, T-shirts with pictures of the temples on them.

I was looking around for Lulu. I had imagined it would be easy to find her once we got to the temples. Now it seemed impossible, with all these people, like at a huge carnival. But I should probably get out and walk around to look for her. What kind of trouble was she in?

"I kind of expected the temples to be different," I said to Ayo, worried about Lulu. "Like, isolated and holy."

She looked serious. "Too many people, yes, but also not fair to keep them away." Then she smiled. "But we are different, because of the road we take."

Before I could ask what she meant, the blonde said, "I can't be seen like this!" She was frantically running her fingers through her drooping hair. In the bright light her face was pouchy without makeup, and very wrinkled. "What will people think of me without my clothes and makeup?"

"Don't worry. The foreign tourists don't understand.

You are privileged, because you came this way," Sai explained. "You might even be allowed to enter the most sacred part of the temple, where most people can't go."

"I don't know. . . ." Lep said. Ayo frowned.

The blonde wasn't listening to Lep. "What the tourists think *does* worry me!" she answered Sai, as if entering the sacred part of the temple didn't matter at all. "I'm a mess. I wish I'd taken the bus!"

Ayo's frown deepened. "Then you would get nothing from the temples. And you still probably won't," she said coldly, turning away from the blonde.

"I'd *buy* some clothes and makeup if I had any money," the blonde grumbled. "Can anybody lend me—" Then she grimaced, knowing that none of us had enough money to lend her anything.

The *gwian* parking lot was small and deserted, the music and voices distant now. The stalls and musicians in the central field were for the rich people who had come by bus. We stopped at an old stone wall topped by sharp spikes, about eight feet high. There was a small gatehouse with a uniformed guard inside and soldiers with guns beside an ornate metal gate. Oddly, the soldiers saluted Lep. He saluted them back.

When the guard in the gatehouse saw Lep, his face broke into a broad grin. "Greetings, Lep! I am happy every time you make it back through the jungle again. And with Madam Ayo," he said, seeing her now. He bowed his head to her. "Very good luck today—a priestess returns."

Then the guard saw the blonde. He glanced back and forth between her and Lep, puzzled, not knowing what to say.

"This trip was difficult," Lep said.

He didn't need to explain to the guard, whose eyes had gone back to the blonde now. "I see," he said, looking worried. He knew it was dangerous to bring a foreigner on the *gwian* track, even though she didn't look rich right now, dirty and bedraggled in her bandit clothes.

The guard was confused. "Lep, you have earned great respect here, and so we trust the passengers you bring. Normally. But this is very perturbing." His voice faded.

The boltzmon again? We were almost there. If only the blonde wouldn't do anything to get him riled up! I had to get inside, to save Lulu and my own life.

"Yes, I know the policy," Lep said. "Only Arterians in the Inner Sanctum." Now Lep seemed worried, too.

"What do you mean, only Arterians?" the blonde wanted to know. "Look at all the foreigners over there."

"Not in here, madam," said the guard. "The Inner Sanctum is only for Arterians who take the jungle track on a *gwian*. It doesn't cost money to enter. What it costs is the courage to come that way."

Where was thirteen-year-old Lulu? I should be looking for her. But I didn't move. I had to get in here. And I wanted the blonde to go in, too. I somehow knew it was necessary for her and me to be together in this place.

And now that the blonde was being told she couldn't enter the sacred part of the temples, she suddenly decided she cared about it after all. Lulu again. "It didn't say that in my guidebook," she argued, as if the guard cared what her guidebook said. "And I *did* take the jungle track. Are the famous temples prejudiced against foreigners?"

The guard looked unhappy. "This is very problematic. I will have to ask the soldiers to escort you away."

The blonde pursed her lips and stuck her chin out, just like Lulu would. Two armed soldiers approached.

Please don't implode! Please don't implode! I was silently begging the guard.

"Wait," Lep said. "She made the trip more dangerous, yes. But if she wasn't on the bridge, we wouldn't have made it. I say she has earned the right to enter." He turned to Ayo. "What do you think?"

The guard watched Ayo. Her opinion was what counted, since she was a priestess here. And she had just chastised the blonde because she cared more about her appearance than the sacred part of the temples. "Well?" Ayo asked her.

"Well what?" the blonde said, looking uncomfortable.

"Why do you want to enter the Inner Sanctum, and the

Crypt? I cannot say what I think until I know how you feel."

Awn had said that many foreigners came to the temples because they thought the temples would give them youth. If anybody had that motivation, it would be the blonde, who—according to the boltzmon immigration officer—was prematurely aged. But that was not a reason that Ayo or the guard would accept. Did the blonde have a deep enough mind to come up with something that would satisfy them? I doubted it.

Suddenly the blonde didn't seem uncomfortable, she seemed sad. Not angry, not irritable, not pushy . . . sad.

"I need answers," she said slowly. "I've been to all the other holy places—Jerusalem, Mecca, Rome, Lourdes. Because something's wrong with my life. Something's been wrong for a long time—and I don't know what it is. Those places didn't help me understand enough to change things. Then I remembered my brother told me about this place."

If this was Lulu, then, of course, I was her brother. She hadn't recognized me; I was too young, and I was dressed like an Arterian. And the me on this Earth had told her about the Time Temples? Did he want her to come here, because something important had to happen here? He must have known more about Arteria than I had, because on this world Arteria was real.

"And then my brother died, all those years ago," the blonde said.

I had seen it happen, but I still felt cold when she said it.

The blonde looked hard at Ayo, then at the guard. Then she slumped a little, wiping one eye. "Years went by, and nothing worked, and then I remembered what he said. So I came to Arteria. But if I don't get into this part of the temples, it'll just be another tourist trap. I went through a lot to come to the temples; I did it the hard way. If you don't let me in . . . I'm afraid there's no place left. Anywhere."

She paused and looked away, embarrassed. "I know this is it, because of what the people on this trip, in this cart, are like. They understand something; they have some kind of peace that I don't have. At first I thought they were just stupid. Now . . ." Her voice faded.

Once again, I had to give her credit. That was more than I expected of her. If she was Lulu, she still had most of Lulu's problems. But at least in all this time she had learned something was wrong.

For a moment no one spoke. If she didn't get in, and thirteen-year-old Lulu didn't get in either, was there any point in my going in? Then the event that would save my life would never happen.

"Knowing there is a problem, that is the first step," Ayo

said. "Most of the rich foreigners like you do not know that. I think . . ." She looked at the guard. "I say yes."

"Well, Madam Ayo." The guard was doubtful, his hand on his chin. "This has never happened before. Very unprecedented." He sighed and briefly closed his eyes. "If it was anybody but Ayo and Lep, I'd say no." He shook his finger at the blonde. "You be careful in there, woman. Behave, do what they say. Because if anything goes wrong, then it'll be on my shoulders. Go! Hurry, before I change my mind." He waved us inside.

The soldiers pulled open the heavy gate and the *gwian* rolled through, into the Inner Sanctum. They shut the gate with a clang and locked it behind us.

And I remembered again that Lep's sister had died because of coming here.

chapter 15

Suddenly it seemed as if all the crowds of tourists had vanished. In here it was quiet, with only the sound of water over stones; in here it felt isolated. It was shady under the trees. We were the only ones here.

We were enclosed on three sides by the stone wall, and the fourth side was the central temple facade—the side of the temple that was forbidden to tourists. One of the smaller temples also stood inside the enclosure. The stream that passed by the front of the temples flowed through here, too, under an archway in the wall. I glanced casually at it from the *gwian*, which was jerking in a funny way.

And then I choked, feeling sick. I put my hand to my mouth. The water in the stream was going too slow. It was frothing over the stones but almost frozen; you had to stare hard at a stone to see the water moving past it at all. Then suddenly it was normal. Then too fast, a blur. And then oozing backward.

"The water!" I said. "What's wrong with the water?"

Lep was guiding Bom-bom to the right-hand wall, on the other side of the small tower, just as though nothing was wrong. But Bom-bom moved in waves, flowing forward quickly, then almost stopping. That was why the *gwian* was jerking.

"It's not the water," Ayo answered me. "It is the earth the water is running through. That's why the temples were built in this place. Time is different here, on the earth itself, and below it. You will understand when you step off the *gwian*."

Did I even *want* to step off the *gwian*? Maybe I just wanted to get out of here.

Lep parked the *gwian* by the wall and hopped off. With lightning speed he unfastened Bom-bom's harness. In slow motion, he draped it over his seat.

"It will take time for you to get used to it," Ayo droned, climbing off the *gwian*, her voice dropping in pitch, like a tape played too slow.

I climbed carefully down, my legs shaky. I held on to the *gwian*. I looked at the stream.

It seemed completely normal.

I turned and backed away from the *gwian*. Now it was

Awn and Sai and the blonde who were speeding up and slowing down as they moved toward the front of it. The blonde's face was set in its barely controlled frantic look.

"You understand?" Ayo asked me. "When you are within the temple time field, the Inner Sanctum, standing on the earth, you don't feel it—not up here, where it is very mild. Everything is relative. It gets stronger deep down in the Crypt. That is where the important things happen—*if* they happen."

I looked away from the *gwian*—I didn't like watching them get off so strangely. I studied the smaller tower. There seemed to be no door in it, only the statues of demons with big teeth, covered with glittering pieces of glass. "You can't go in this thing?" I asked her.

"Only the main temple has an inside—and this is the only way to get to it. Most of the people who come to the temples just climb up and down the balconies on the outside. The fee they pay keeps the temples in repair."

The doorway to the main temple was the huge open mouth of a demon, with wide staring eyes and a black mustache. Three women dressed all in white with red umbrellas like Ayo emerged from it. They lifted their arms in welcome, and Ayo ran to them, but they did not embrace. They spoke their joyous greetings in hushed voices.

Then they saw the blonde and looked shocked. They

whispered anxiously with Ayo, red umbrellas clustered above them. The blonde was watching them as intensely as I was. I thought about dying forty years ago.

I had to ask her. I couldn't put it off any longer.

"Lulu?" I said, experimentally.

The blonde almost jumped out of her skin. "When did I tell you my name?" she said. She turned to Awn and Sai. "I never told anybody my name, did I?"

"No, you didn't," Lep said. He had joined us now that Bom-bom was comfortably grazing. "I thought it was strange. But you never did."

"How do you know my name?" the blonde demanded. She seemed angry, but maybe it was just because she was scared.

"Because I'm Chris," I said. "Your brother."

She tilted her head to the side, her brow furrowed. "Hello?" she said sarcastically. "My brother was two years younger than me, and American."

"Well, I'm still only eleven, but I *am* Chris," I said. "I'm just dressed like an Arterian. Don't you remember how I looked when I was eleven, from pictures?"

"You expect me to *believe* this?" she said.

"I did notice you have a funny accent, like a foreigner," Lep said. "But I didn't like to say anything about it. People have reasons for their secrets."

"I can prove who I am," I said to the blonde. "Dad gave

you a Prada bag, and you kept cosmetics and jewelry in it. You and Dad played golf a lot. Your room was the whole third floor, and everything was pink. You had parties up there, and I had to ask you to turn down the music. When you lied about me at school, and Mom broke up your party, you gave a pep talk that turned the whole school against me." I didn't say anything about my death; I wasn't sure I wanted to yet. "You hated me from the beginning, and I never knew why." I paused, staring hard at her. "And now, here we are. And I'm still eleven, and you're grown-up."

The blonde's mouth had dropped open.

"And he saved your life," Lep told her. "The bandits would have eaten you if he didn't make us both risk our lives to save you."

Suddenly she was laughing hysterically. "You . . . Chris saved my life? Oh, and after what *I* did to . . ." Then she pulled herself together and shook her head. "Impossible," she said. "The whole thing's impossible. Just because you know that stuff doesn't mean that—"

"Excuse me," Ayo interrupted her. The three women in white were just behind her. "Something very strange. I don't know if it's a good thing that you were allowed to enter the Inner Sanctum after all."

"*Now* what?" the blonde said, sounding irritable; but now I knew it meant only that she was scared again.

"The sisters tell me . . . you are here already. Down in the Crypt."

"What's *that* supposed to mean?" the blonde said.

"Is she thirteen years old?" I asked them, suddenly hopeful.

They looked puzzled. "Yes, that is her real-time age. How did you know that?" they asked me.

"Er, I always knew she came here when she was thirteen. She just appeared out of nowhere, right?"

"Yes, she did. Two days ago," said the oldest priestess. "It was very frightening. But we have been keeping her down there; her appearance was such a mystery we felt it was meant to be."

"I don't know what any of you are talking about," the blonde objected.

"But if the girl in the Crypt is only thirteen, then how did you know this woman was her as soon as you saw her?" I asked them. "She's changed so much."

"You'll understand in the Crypt," Ayo said. "But it won't be safe for either of you."

"Hold it. Just wait a minute," the blonde said. She turned to me. "You *did* just pop out of existence, back in the bandit camp. I saw it with my own eyes. If you could do something impossible like that, then maybe you could also do something else impossible, like be Chris, still alive." She was breathing heavily, staring at me. "And eleven, the same age as when you . . ." she said hoarsely, her eyes losing focus.

"I said he was a wizard," Lep murmured. "He denied it then. Now we know."

"I'm Chris," I said. "You wrecked my sand castle. Mom was always telling Dad he spoiled you. She said he shouldn't give you expensive, pretentious gifts like—"

"Okay, okay, spare me the sordid details," the blonde said, wiping her eyes. She turned to Ayo. "Are you telling me they might not let us go down there. After all *this?*"

The three priestesses were older than Ayo, one elderly, two middle-aged. They whispered together.

I knew it was true now. There was a Lulu on this planet, and a Lulu on Earth. There had been a Chris on this planet, just like the one on Earth. But this world was forty years ahead. Lulu was forty years older here—and I had died on this world forty years ago, when I was eleven. Just like I would die on our world, very soon, if I didn't fix things here at the temples.

The priestesses broke out of their huddle, and the oldest priestess said, "It will be very dangerous to go down to the Crypt now—for you two especially, and the young one who is already there."

The blonde stuck out her chin. "But after all this, you've *got* to—"

The old priestess lifted her hand to silence her. "You must learn patience," she said. "I hadn't finished speaking. I was saying, it will be very dangerous if you go down. But the convergence of events is so unusual—even miraculous—that we must let it take its course. We would be presuming too much authority if we tried to interfere. And now I must explain about the Crypt, for those of you who have not been there before."

Even the blonde was listening raptly.

"The Crypt contains images of your lives—the past and the future. The images of the past are unchanging, they have happened already and cannot be altered by human beings at this place. But the images of your futures are only possibilities. Sometimes they can change—depending on whether or not *you* can change. Do you understand?"

We all nodded. I would have liked to ask some questions, but somehow I didn't dare.

"Come. We will go now."

We all followed the priestesses toward the giant demon-mouth doorway. I was in the back, beside Lep—the blonde was right behind the priestesses, of course. I had about one million questions, but what I asked him was, "Do you go down to the Crypt every time you come here?"

He nodded.

"What . . . what does it do for you?"

"Everybody has his own reasons for coming here—the

few who are allowed. Coming here is why I believed I could help you save her from the bandits." He paused. "I also come to see my sister, in the past," Lep added.

"You said she died—*because* she came here."

He nodded solemnly. "She saw her future, and after that, she did not *want* to live any longer. She did not believe she could change it. Soon after, she ended her life. That is one of the dangers of coming here." He paused and looked away from me. "I think about it all the time. I wish I had been able to save her. When we were here together I did not take control; I did not make her believe that she could change her life."

"You mean . . . it doesn't happen automatically? A person has to be convinced, a person has to *decide* to change?"

He sighed. "I will blame myself forever, because I didn't do the right things here to help her change."

And *I* would die if I didn't do the right things to help thirteen-year-old Lulu change. But I had no idea what I could do. She never listened to me. She was as stubborn as a rock. For a second I gripped Lep's arm. "But what can you *do* to help somebody change?" I asked him, my voice rising.

He looked at me sadly. "I cannot tell you that. It is different for every person."

And now, even though we had all made it here, I was more frightened than ever.

We crossed the old stone bridge over the stream. The

railing was carved with grotesque grinning stone faces, worn smooth over the years. Over by the wall Bom-bom grazed in the dappled sunlight.

The priestesses closed their umbrellas and stepped through the dark temple doorway, framed by sharp triangular red demon's teeth. The blonde, right behind them, did not hesitate an instant—she was a very desperate woman. Awn and Sai, holding hands, paused briefly before they entered. Lep walked calmly through, but I stopped. I wanted to get to Lulu, but at the same time I was terrified of what she would do. I couldn't imagine her in this situation, but I knew she could turn it into a nightmare if she wanted to. And then I would die for sure.

I stepped inside and caught up with Lep.

chapter 16

The corridor turned away from the sunlight as soon as we entered, and suddenly it was dark. Little round metal lamps hung from the arched ceiling and burned in sconces on the walls. They were oil lamps, from the smell of it. In their feeble, flickering light, I could see that the paintings on the walls and ceiling were blackened with all the smoke from over the centuries. The paintings were so dark, you couldn't really make out what the people and buildings were, only that they were done in a strange, primitive style.

We followed the rustle of the priestesses' robes. They passed several doorways. Soon we came to a stone spiral staircase, so steep and narrow we had to walk in single file. There was no railing.

And then we heard the painful screaming, garbled and echoing at first, but growing clearer as we descended. "No, no, no! It's not going to happen like that. That's wrong, it's all wrong!"

Lulu, no doubt about it. Had she been screaming like that for two days, since the boltzmon had sent her here?

I bumped into Lep. I peered down, craning my head to see around the corner. The blonde must have stopped. Had she recognized her own thirteen-year-old voice?

"Come," I heard one of the priestesses urge her. "It is too late to go back now."

We moved down toward the screaming. The stairway ended at a small room with an old metal door. There was barely space for the nine of us to squeeze together. All the Arterians bowed their heads, their palms pressed together against their foreheads. I did it, too, just for good luck. When I looked up, I saw that even the blonde was doing it.

The old priestess pushed open the door and beckoned us inside. We could see through the open door that the light inside was flickering, not like the lamplight but like an old-time movie. The others moved slowly inside, past the priestesses, who did not enter. I followed.

It was impossible to tell what shape the room was, or even how large it was, because all of the surfaces were reflective, like the sharpest mirrors I had ever seen. The five of us entering were reflected around the room. But we weren't the same in all the reflections. In many of them we were different ages.

In the middle of the room stood thirteen-year-old Lulu in her little short cheerleader's skirt, her white sneakers, her letter sweater with pom-poms. Her thick lipstick and eye makeup were smeared, her hair greasy and tousled.

"Chris! Oh, Chris!" Lulu cried out when she saw me in the open doorway, her face lighting up.

She started toward me, frantic. "Oh, Chris, we've got to get out of here! This is a nightmare. Those ladies in white keep telling me I'm not going crazy, but it's still a nightmare here. I never thought I'd be so happy to see—"

Just before the door behind us clanged shut, she got a good look at the blonde, and stopped. Her smile fell away, replaced by an expression of disgust. "What are *you* doing here?" she said to the blonde. She turned to me, pointing at the blonde. "I'll never be like her, I'll never be that person, even though I keep seeing myself turning into her, over and over again. It's a lie. It *has* to be a lie! This place lies. Most of all it lies about . . . about what happens to you, Chris."

"Be quiet!" Lep ordered her. "It's dangerous to speak that way in here—very dangerous."

"How do *you* know?" Lulu said contemptuously, taking in his appearance.

"He's been here over and over again," I said. "And he knows a lot about everything. More than you do."

"What's wrong with you, Chris? You're talking funny. Just get me out of here so we can go home. Now!"

I ignored her order. We moved into the room, watching our various reflections. I saw Lep as a child, Lep as he was now, Lep as an old man. I saw all versions of the others, too—and I saw Sai start to cry with happiness and hug Awn when she saw herself as an old woman. Maybe she was sick and had come here to see if she would survive her illness.

I also saw myself as a baby, a toddler, and as I was now.

But there were no older versions of me.

In the room, and in the reflections—it was sometimes a little hard to tell which was which—the blonde approached Lulu. "What's the matter with me? Why do you hate me so much? How did you turn into me?"

"Look around," Lulu said. "There's all different versions, but they all end the same. And Chris . . ." Her voice broke; she couldn't go on. Lulu crying about me, for real? That was a new one.

There was Lulu jumping around as a cheerleader, Lulu inhaling her first cigarette and getting sick, Lulu screaming at me, her face distorted with rage. Strangely, Lulu as an adult was always alone—driving alone, sitting at a desk alone, watching television alone.

And there was me at the computer, me walking home from school, me falling from the fire department tower. The kids shouted and then silently ran away. I lay crumpled on the ground. It made me cringe to see it.

"I didn't know they would do that!" Lulu screamed. "I didn't know they were crazy!" the blonde screamed at the same time.

And then the blonde added softly, "That's when everything changed."

I was in the hospital, hooked up to all sorts of machines. Mom and Dad were crying. "Lulu, you've got to go to the Time Temples in Arteria," I managed to mumble.

"Shhh," Mom said gently. "Don't waste your energy."

And then Mom and Dad were crying at the funeral. Lulu wasn't crying.

I glanced only briefly at the Arterians, absorbed in their own reflections. They were not alone in their reflections. People who must have been friends and family were with them. But Lulu's adult self seemed to have no friends or relatives.

"I'm not going to be like that, alone all the time!" Lulu protested. "Why does it keep showing that? Why does it keep showing you dying?"

"Isn't it obvious?" I said to Lulu and the blonde, too. "You turned out that way because of hate. And I died because of your hate, too. Why do you hate me so much?" I asked them. "Maybe that's the answer. Maybe things will change if you stop hating. I never understood your hate. I still don't."

"Why are you talking like this?" Lulu said, sounding close to tears again. "You never talked like this before."

"I've been through a lot since before. Maybe I learned something. Why do you hate me?"

Lulu and the blonde looked away from each other, thinking. "You were an embarrassment," the blonde said.

"Right," said Lulu. "You're so weird and out of it, I'm embarrassed to be in the same family with you. You make my life miserable. Why shouldn't I hate you for that?"

"You were always running to Mom for everything, instead of standing up for yourself," the blonde said. "But . . . you don't seem that way now. Maybe that's why I didn't recognize you. Like you said, you changed on this trip. You saved my life."

"He *what?*" Lulu said.

"He risked his life to save me. After what I did to him. He's changed, all right."

"Are you *sure?*" Lulu said suspiciously.

"Okay, I changed. But me being weird—is that the *only* reason you hate me?" I asked her. I remembered what Lep said, about how he hadn't said the right things in here, and then his sister had died. I had to force myself to be tough now, or *I'd* die. "Me being weird doesn't seem like enough. Wasn't there something else I did to make you hate me so much? Watch for it. Maybe you'll see it."

Lulu before I was born. Mom and Dad playing with her, cuddling her, both of them devoting all their attention to her. "Isn't she beautiful? Isn't she smart? See how well she walks at her age! See how talented she is!" And Lulu beamed and ran to them with open arms.

And then me as an infant, Mom holding me, Lulu pulling at Mom's leg, then opening her arms, wanting to hold me, and Mom pushing her away. "Leave me alone, Lulu, I'm busy with Chris!" Mom shouted at her. Lulu went away and cried alone. Again, Lulu trying to hold me after taking me on the walk, and Mom pulling me out of her arms.

The beach. To my surprise, the sand castle I was building was *not* so primitive, as I assumed later; it was beautiful, detailed, imaginative, and Mom and Dad made a very big deal over it. I gloated, and said, "And all Lulu can make is upside-down buckets." When Mom and Dad left, Lulu kicked the castle down.

"You deserved it!" Lulu and the blonde said simultaneously. And maybe I did. I didn't remember being so obnoxious.

Me at six, already writing on the computer. We had only one then. Lulu, eight, pushed me away from it. But she could only fumble with it, making mistakes, accidentally deleting things. Mom ordered her away from the machine. I glanced smugly at her and sat down at the keyboard again.

Dad, an artist himself, impressed by my drawings. He didn't notice Lulu's lousy drawings, much worse than mine even though she was two years older. He took her to the golf course with him. But at that age she was bored there, and he angrily told her to behave.

"I never knew," I said. "I never knew that's how it was for you."

"Well, now you do!" they both snapped, still speaking eerily together.

Despite everything she had done, I began to feel sorry for her.

"You took my parents away from me," Lulu said. "And you were always better than me at everything they cared about. And a weirdo, too. How could I *not* hate you?"

An infant, I crawled toward Lulu. Impulsively she picked me up and hugged me and rocked me, smiling, her expression unusually peaceful. Years later I gave her a valentine. She took it up to her room and saved it.

Those were the good times I hadn't remembered. "Why couldn't it be like that more?" I asked Lulu. "That way, things might work out."

"And he didn't take our parents away on purpose," the blonde told her. "I can see that now. He wanted you to love him. And maybe you can. He's changed now; he got strong or tough or something. Maybe . . . maybe you can change, too."

"Why should I change?" Lulu said, pouting.

"Because you don't want to turn into me," said the blonde. "You said so yourself. You looked at me with disgust. But mainly because . . . you don't want Chris to die because of you." She was crying now. "That's what really messed up my life."

"But *how* do you change? I don't know how to change!" Lulu said, stamping her foot.

At that instant I caught a glimpse of a young man I hadn't seen before. "See that guy?" I asked them, pointing. "You ever see him before?"

"No," Lulu said.

"He . . . he looks like you," murmured the blonde.

My heart lifted. "And I never saw him before, I never got that old—until Lulu just now asked how to change."

"You . . . you died at eleven," the blonde said. "Those horrible kids—"

"I changed. And if Lulu can change, too . . . maybe I won't die then."

The Arterians had left. They must have found what they wanted already. How long had we been here? There was no way to tell.

"Nobody answered *me*!" Lulu said. "How do you change? So I won't be like you. Always alone. And so Chris . . . Chris won't die."

"Knowing there is a problem is the first step," the blonde said, quoting what Ayo had said to her.

"I didn't take Mom and Dad away from you," I said. "They love you as much as ever, and Dad cares about you a lot more than me."

"What are you talking about?"

"You know he does. You can see it. Look, there he is buying you the Prada bag, there he is fixing up your room. Did he do that for me? There he is showing off your golf swing to his friends."

"Okay, but . . . I'll still be embarrassed to be your sister."

"Not anymore," the blonde said. "He's been through a lot now. And he saved my life. He's not the Chris I remember. You're lucky you had this chance. You better appreciate it. If only I'd had the chance, back when . . ." She wiped her eye. "Well, I got here anyway. Better late than never, I guess. But it won't bring my Chris back."

Now adult Lulu was having lunch with another woman. She was on a boat with a group of people, laughing. She didn't look so ugly anymore. She looked almost pretty when she was riding in a car with a man. There was a warmth I had seen in her smile only once before—the time she was rocking me as an infant.

"Look," I said to the blonde. "That . . . that must be your child you're holding."

"I never had a child," the blonde said. She was crying again. "I'm too old now." She looked at Lulu. "But . . . but now maybe you will. If you can change." She could barely get the words out.

Now I was there all over the place, as a middle-aged man, as an old man, not in just one reflection. Was it possible Lulu *was* going to change? I never would have thought she could.

But then, I had never imagined a place like this, either. And Lulu had been in here for two days already, watching all this over and over again. That must be partly why she was willing to change without putting up more of a fight. This place was pretty powerful, all right, as I had written on the map, without understanding a thing.

The reflections blurred, they began to shrink, they faded. In a moment we were standing in a small room with bare stone walls, lit by oil lamps.

"I guess that means it's time to go," I said, wiping my forehead. I hadn't realized I was sweating.

"But I still don't know how to change," Lulu complained.

"You could start by leaving Chris alone," the blonde said. She sniffed. "You could start by thinking about somebody else and not just yourself. That's what *I* saw here. That's why I still have some hope. I found out something, too, and it might not be too late." She nudged Lulu. "And like I said, you won't be embarrassed by him anymore. That will help a lot."

And that's when it hit me. The boltzmon had orchestrated this thing, step by step. If it hadn't put the blonde in the *gwian,* I never would have had the chance to save her life, and that had made a big difference. If it hadn't ridden the *gwian* out onto the bridge, the blonde would never have proved her courage, and that had made a big difference, too.

And if it hadn't tossed Lulu into this room, I still would have died in the next few days.

Sure, the boltzmon made mistakes, too. But I was beginning to see that it might not be completely indifferent to me, as it claimed. Why had it done all this if it didn't care, if its purpose hadn't been to help me after all?

The old priestess poked her head into the room. "I think you are finished now," she said.

chapter 17

Outside the sun was rising over the chasm. Lulu groaned with relief. "It's so great to be out of there!" She glanced around indifferently at the temples. "Weird," she said. Then she stared into a tiny piece of reflective glass in the small temple, patting her hair into place.

"Is it the next morning?" I asked Ayo, who came out with us.

"Two days later," she said. She didn't ask what had happened inside. Maybe she could tell.

The *gwian* wasn't there. "Where's Lep?" I asked her.

"Camping, on the other side of the village." She turned to the blonde. "He and the others are waiting for you, if you want to go back through the jungle with him."

"You mean he'll take me back again, after all the trouble I caused?" the blonde said.

"You can take the bus if you prefer. We can get a ticket for you."

"No, no," the blonde said, laughing. "It's Lep, if he'll take me. Going that way—that's the whole point."

"He has your Prada bag," Ayo said, smiling back. "But . . . he would prefer if you did not take it into the jungle. There are other bandits."

The blonde made a gesture of dismissal. "Who needs it?" she said.

"Your Prada bag?" Lulu said, amazed. "You don't want it? Can I have it?"

"Don't get too caught up in that stuff," the blonde cautioned her. "That was part of what happened to me."

"I'll get caught up in whatever I want!" Lulu said, pouting again.

The blonde and I turned and looked at each other, then back to Lulu. We didn't say a word.

"Well, I guess the bag doesn't matter *that* much," Lulu muttered, looking at the ground.

"It won't be easy. Just never forget what you saw in that room," the blonde told her. "Ayo. Or, I mean, Madam Ayo. Where is Lep's campsite?"

"On the other side of the village behind the temples. There's only one street, very short, and the campground is just beyond."

"I'm off," the blonde said. "Don't want to keep them waiting any longer." She turned to us, her expression very serious, even kind. "Thanks, Chris, for everything. And good luck, you two. Don't forget me, Lulu, and don't forget what you saw in the temple." She turned and started for the gate.

"We're going with you," I said. "Lulu and I want to ride the *gwian*, too."

"Huh?" Lulu said.

Ayo put her hand on my arm. "I think you have another way to go home."

"I do?" I said.

"You must know. You have been away and come back again since I met you."

I had an idea. "But why can't I say good-bye to Lep and the others first?"

"It will only make it more difficult for you to leave," she said.

"Well, maybe," I admitted. I would miss Lep a lot. And I was pretty sure I would never see him again. Maybe it was better to just go home.

" 'Bye!" the blonde called out, waving as she walked to the gate. She seemed different. She was even standing up straighter now.

I bowed to Ayo. "Thank you for everything," I said.

"That's not enough, I know. We can never thank you enough. So much has happened here. I don't know what to say."

I prodded Lulu's sneaker with my foot. For a moment she didn't understand. Then she said, "Oh, yeah. Thanks. I think . . . maybe things will be better now."

"That is all the thanks we need. Good luck." Ayo turned and entered the temple.

"Come on." I started for the gate and the gatehouse.

"So how *are* we going to get back?" Lulu wanted to know. "What were you talking about? Where in the world are we, anyway?"

"Not on Earth. On a different Earth. It's the same as ours, except it has a country on it called Arteria, and that's where we are. It's just like what you used to call the 'useless' country I made up on my computer," I couldn't resist pointing out. "And this planet is forty years *ahead* of our Earth in time; that's why you're grown-up here."

She stopped, grimacing at me. "Yeah, but . . . I mean, how did we get here? What's going on, anyway? How are we getting home?"

"Remember at your slumber party on Saturday?" I said. It seemed like a million years ago to me, and probably to her, too. "You saw something weird in my pocket?"

"Oh, yeah," she said slowly. "And you kept trying to hide it from me."

"Well, it's hard to explain what it is. It's called the boltzmon. It knows everything that ever happened and everything that ever will happen. It brought me here, it brought you here, and it did things to help along the way. And it can take us home."

She shook her head. "I wouldn't believe any of this, except . . . it's really happening. You still have that thing in your pocket?"

I shook my head. "But I think I know where we can find it. Come on. If I prod you with my foot, be really rude to the guard, okay?"

"Huh? You *want* me to be rude?"

"One last time. Nobody's better at it than you. That's how you have to deal with the boltzmon."

The guardhouse was on the other side of the gate. The soldiers swung it open as we passed. The same guard was there as when we entered. I hoped he was still the boltzmon.

"Hi," I said to him.

The guard looked very surprised to see Lulu coming out of the Inner Sanctum, since he had not let her in through the gate. "Hey! How'd you get in there?" he said, sounding angry already. That was a good sign.

"You brought my sister directly here from America," I said, "and you know it."

"You are talking nonsense! It is very perturbing. We

are in great danger if someone could get in there past me."

As soon as he said "perturbing" I prodded Lulu's foot.

"Your security stinks," Lulu said. "Piece of cake."

He leaned forward, gripping the half door of the gatehouse with both hands. "How dare you speak to me like that? I should have you two urchins arrested. This is the most perturbing thing that has happened to me in years!"

"Why do you keep saying 'perturbing'?" Lulu asked him. "That's a stupid word."

"Yeah, get perturbed," I said. "Get perturbed and take us home. Everything's finished, everything's okay now. As if you didn't know."

"Your tie is crooked," Lulu pointed out. "It looks really stupid."

"I AM VERY PERTURBED!" he roared.

Everything flickered and went black.

chapter 18

We were standing on the sidewalk in front of our house in the late afternoon.

"That's funny. It usually brings me back inside," I said.

I was holding the ash in my hand. I slipped it into my pocket.

"What are we going to tell Mom and Dad?" Lulu said.

"We'll have to play it by ear. I don't know how long we've been missing. I never know exactly what moment it's going to bring me back to. Maybe they'll be at work."

We walked up to the front door. "Gee, I never noticed how much the house needs painting," I said.

"When did the glass in the window get cracked?" Lulu said. "And it's so dirty."

I had trouble unlocking the door, the key was stiff in the lock, but I finally managed. The door squeaked as I pulled it open. It had never done that before.

We stepped into the front hall. The new carpet was threadbare; on the stairway it was worn all the way through to the wood. "What's going on?" I whispered, beginning to be really scared.

"Who's there? Who's coming in here?" an aged, frightened voice called out.

We walked into the living room. An old man stood in front of the easy chair; an old woman sat on the couch. They both looked terrified.

What was going on? "Oh, uh, sorry," I said. "We thought this was our house." And it *was* our house—except everything about it was too old.

The old man and woman didn't speak. They just stared at us, their mouths hanging open.

Then I saw the pictures on the mantel. Lulu and me, just about the ages we were right now.

"Are you . . . ghosts?" the old man said, his voice shaking.

"There's no such thing as ghosts," the old woman said. "It's some kind of terrible trick. finding kids who look just like our children did when they disappeared. Why are you doing this?" she asked us angrily. "Did they pay you? Who sent you here?"

Now I understood. I took the ash out of my pocket. "You brought us back too late! A whole, whole lot too late!"

Huh? The boltzmon sounded confused. *Oh, yeah, now I see. I forgot to jump back to your planet's present time. But it's only forty years later than the night you left. Just a blink of the eye to me.*

"But it's a lifetime to us! Bring us back to the same night I left, and upstairs, too."

"He's talking to himself," the old man mumbled.

"Go away, just leave now!" cried the old woman, her voice cracking. "I can't bear the sight of you!"

"See what you've done to them?" I said to the boltzmon.

I understand now. This is a very perturbing situation.

The world trembled and went black.

chapter 19

We were in my room at night. The ash was not in my hand.

"It's gone," I whispered.

But there wasn't time for me to feel disappointed that my adventures might be over. I looked at the desk clock. It was midnight. I hoped it was the same night I had left the last time.

I put my finger to my lips. Lulu seemed too disoriented to do much anyway. I crept out to the hallway and listened. The carpeting was new again.

"Thank you," I heard Dad say, as he hung up the phone.

"Still no sign of her," Mom said. It was not a question.

"No sign," Dad said. "And the longer she's gone, the less . . ." He couldn't finish.

I sneaked back into the room. "Great. It's the night we disappeared. I came back earlier—they think I'm asleep in here. You've been missing since cheerleading."

"What am I going to tell them?" She wasn't being hostile or blaming me, as she normally would have in a situation like this. She was asking me for advice. Maybe I really had changed. And maybe she was changing, too.

"There's no way you're not going to get in trouble," I said. "They were mad at me, and I came home a lot earlier. They've already checked out all your friends. They have the cops looking for you. You're going to have to say you were alone, or with people they don't know about."

She scowled at me, getting angry now. "It's all your fault, you and that stupid blitzman, or whatever it is."

"Stop it, Lulu. If this didn't happen, I'd be dead in a few days. And you'd turn into that blonde woman, ugly and alone. This little problem is *nothing* compared to those things."

She sighed. "Okay, okay, you're right."

"You're going to have to get on the PA system at morning announcements tomorrow and take back what you said in your pep talk about me being an embarrassment to everybody in the school. Then they won't try to make me climb those stairs."

"I'll do what I can. But you have to do something, too. If you really did get tougher, you can stand up to them better if they still try something."

She was right about that. And I believed I could do it, too.

"So what are we going to do right now?" she wanted to know.

"The sooner you show up, the better, the less angry they'll be. You can say you climbed up the tree to sneak upstairs."

"I guess . . . I'll say I was with some girls they don't know, whose parents were out of town. We were watching videos and forgot what time it was."

"That's probably the best you can do," I told her. "They'll ground you, for sure. And probably other things, too. But like I said, it could be a lot worse. Go on, get it over with."

"You're not coming with me?" She looked down at the floor. "I'd . . . I'd feel better if you did."

I didn't know what I could do to make it less painful. But she had never asked me for help with them before. "Sure," I said.

We walked out of the room. It was the first time we had been united in a problem with our parents, and not against each other.

I hoped it was a sign of things to come.

I hadn't had a chance to thank the boltzmon for fixing our lives, and now it was gone.

Would I ever see it again?

Wouldn't you like to know?